Seven Sins Plus One

Seven Sins Plus One
OBSESSION

COREY LOWE

MILL CITY PRESS

Mill City Press, Inc.
2301 Lucien Way #415
Maitland, FL 32751
407.339.4217
www.millcitypress.net

Due to the changing nature of the Internet, if there are any web addresses, links, or URLs included in this manuscript, these may have been altered and may no longer be accessible. The views and opinions shared in this book belong solely to the author and do not necessarily reflect those of the publisher. The publisher, therefore, disclaims responsibility for the views or opinions expressed within the work.

Paperback ISBN-13: 978-1-6628-3446-2
Ebook ISBN-13: 978-1-6628-3447-9

[NARRATIVE] The twenty year on force vet who was pass over for lead detective by a three-year rookie. The five-time winner of the Miss universe pageant, beaten by a shy, bookworm nobody on her first try. Or the majority of us, those of us who work 9-5 to maintain a decent living, hard worker even two jobs; outshined by the privilege, who throws it in your face. Some people don't see it, some people do, and others simply ignore it, but it's still there… RIVALS… A WORTHY OPPONANT… Weather you admitted or not we all have at least one rival. Some are heathy, friendly, challenging, while others are hateful, treacherous, and vengeful. Being the best, being the first at something, or just being better than a particular person. Believe it or not we all want someone to push us to do better, but there are those of us who take that definition to the limit of obsession... and beyond. Now I know what you think when you hear the word obsession, but don't get ahead of me just yet. How about we get started on this story and I'll come in from time-to-time to persuade you to keep reading. Deal…? Good… Tragedy…

(woman screams in pain) Ahhh!!!! Push Push… Ahhh!!!! Almost there here's the head one more push…Ahhh!!!! Here we go... One moment…hear you are it's a boy… Congratulations ma'am it's a boy.

Get him away from me. Those were the first and last words I ever heard from my mother. She died a few minutes later after I was born, well accorded to the doctors file. You saw the file? Yea, I did and the recorded birth. I see… we'll talk about that later. And what about your father? That's a good question, let's just say he didn't pursue me so I didn't waste my time looking for him. Did you want to; I mean how did you feel after finding out? That's a session for another day, so are we good hear Doc? But were making good progress, are you that eager to go? Don't have a choice its mandatory when you involve in a shootout. People upstairs want to make sure I'm not crazy, drinking my pain away or something. Do you want to tell me about that? There's nothing to tell that you don't already know Doc. It was a raid me and my partner were in, and it was either them or us. Yes, it was my first time taking a life, but it was necessary. Listen Doc I'm fine I'm not climbing walls or spacing out I can still do my job; so can you just sign the form I don't want to be late. That's what I'm afraid of detective…I know you know your fine, but I know your history. No, you don't know my history, because if you did as you claim that sentences wouldn't have come out your mouth. Listen you got my word Doc, if the other shoe ever drops you'll be my first call. Ok detective your word has a good reputation. Now that's something from my past history you do know Doc. Everything up here in this head is nice and quiet… (Keys smiles) What can I say I like the quiet. Now see when you say stuff like that…later Doctor until our next sessions… Mourning mourning and how are we today? Hmmm, is someone in a good mood today detective? Just another day Monroe, good guys catching bad guys and of course talking about my feelings in counseling…you know the usual. Yea let's not make that a habit Keys, you already got eyes on you, you don't need more. Yea I hear you, so what we got today? I got the file in the car, lets' go do our part for the city. The car? Lieutenant put us on this? I asked for it Keys, we been doing missing persons for a few years now. Time for a change to Homicide. You ok with that? Homicide huh? If I didn't know better Monroe one might think you got ulterior motives. Keys you overthink way too much. What can I say partner, it's my specialty. Yea, an annoying one… lets go you're driving Keys. So tell me about this case. Here's the file, unknown male shot to back of the head. I didn't ask for any other details I figure we get all that when we arrive at the scene. Yea I prefer it that way myself Monroe, you know rather than read a file. Exactly…well here we are. I never gotten around to ask Keys, are you good? Yea I'm good… you good Monroe? (Monroe sighs) Hank I wasn't trying to say anything I…I know what you meant Monroe, I'm good, but I appreciate it. Hey Rodgers what we got? Detective Kelly Monroe always good to see you, what you didn't read the file? We already talk about this Rodgers; we prefer the hands on method rather then read it. (Rodgers scoffs) I see you still got your little helper with you. He's my partner Kyle you know that. (Keys cracks a smile) Hank Keys how you doing? Oh I know who you are Keys...excuse me detective Keys. Got a nice ring to it don't it? Rolls of your tongue pretty smooth. (Rodgers grunts with envy)

I wouldn't know I don't hear it. Don't be a smartass Rodgers. It's all good Monroe, wouldn't be in this line of work If I can't handle a little sarcasm. (Rodgers steps up to Keys) Who said I was being sarcastic. All right gentlemen zip it up, if we are all done measuring we got a homicide right in front of us, so can we get back to it? So I ask again, Rodgers what we got? (Rodgers sighs) Male, white late 30s, what appears to be seven gun shots to the back of the head. No gun was found, four credit cards, a picture of him and what looks like his wife and kid, and three hundred dollars left in his wallet. Who found the body? Jogger over there stumble on him on her normal route, freaked out and called it in. Well we can rule out robbery since his wallet is still with him. But where is his ID Rodgers? He could have forgotten or lost it, happen to me a few times. Yea or the killer took it, it's what we have to figure out. Well, body is still warm so I'm thinking a few hours maybe, we'll see what Landers say. Anything else Rodgers? No I'm just a patrolmen bae I just read off the file and contain the area. What's wrong with your man, he hasn't said a word, just staring at the body, don't tell me he's squeamish or something. You see that Kyle that how shit get started and you wonder why we fell off. It's a thing he does I don't know what it is but it works for him. (Monroe smiles) Watch and learn...Keys! Other than his ID he's missing something else...blood. Which tells me this is a secondary scene… body was moved. And Rodgers…these holes didn't all come from a gun either, only this hole came from a gun. (Rodgers angrily grunts) How can you tell that Sherlock? If you look a little closer only this hole has gunshot residue around it, the others seem to be a smoke screen to cover up the one executed shot. This was personal and professional in my opinion. Now I'm just thinking at loud, but I also think the killer wanted the body to be found. Well look at you detective and why do you think that? Well you said that jogger stumble on the body on her normal route? Yea so? 3rd and Maple is one of the most frequent places for runners to jog. And also Monroe said the body was still warm, no more than a few hours dead. That tells us the Unsub commented the murder somewhere nearby and place him here. Which means the killer or killers planed this out, this wasn't body dumb. But like I said Rodgers Its just my opinion, I don't know maybe I'm overthinking things. (Rodgers angrily grunts again) Wow Monroe your partner really knows how to piss me off don't he. Really Unsub, seems like someone been binge watching criminal minds a little too long. (Monroe smiles) In all fairness Rodgers you did ask, but I appreciate it we'll take it from here. Yea, I think that's a good idea… I'll call you later. How you doing Doctor what can you tell us? Follow me to the corners and after I clean him up I can tell you everything. Alright we'll follow you, thanks again Kyle I'll see you later. Yea anytime Kelly… happy hunting little shadow…Preciate it Rodgers. You're not going to ask? Asked what? O you mean what's the deal between you and Rodgers? I figured that you two had history that much was clear, but other than that what you and he had in the past or present is none of my business. (Monroe stares with confusing) Just like that… not the least bit curious? Yea, you should know that about me by now Monroe, I don't get into other people personal business. I figure if you want me to know something you'll tell me. (Monroe sighs) You're definitely one of a kind Hank. With that being said I never gotten around in asking why you stayed in being my partner when everyone else brushed me off? I mean everybody at the department know my…let's say past generation. What changed in you Monroe? There you go again always over thinking things. I don't judge people or their family of what they did in the past. You're your own man, what you do or don't do is your choice and I respect that. (Keys half smiles) Alright… Well let's focus on the present rather than the past and see what the good doctor has to say about the body. Detective Monroe, Keys, seems like you got an interesting John Doe. How so Doctor Lander?

Well I'm just starting to clean him up but I estimate time of Death would be around four hours ago according to liver temp. Body is still semi-warm. Keys You said you thought he was shot? Yea. Well your right, when I took a closer look at the holes, it appears that only this one was a through and through. Here take a look. You see the powder burns? Yea, close up execution. Here you think made the others holes' doctor? Can't say right now I have to open him up and do a full autopsy to know better. When I know more I'll give you a call detective. Alright thank you Dr. Lander. Let's head back to the station Keys and see were the Lieutenant want us to go next. Right behind you partner.

[**NARRATIVE**: you ever had one of those days where you get that feeling like something not right? I mean you wake up, eat breakfast, drink your coffee, go to work, come home, and go to bed. You repeat this day after day. But this day… that Angel and Devil on your shoulder is not just talking to you… they screaming at you.] Here he is Frank Steffens 53. Dr. Landers faxed his dental records and got an ID. Why does that name sound familiar? Gambler what you got on this guy. Well his name is familiar, Frank Steffens, isn't he that lead contractor and co-owner of the new outside mall they building downtown. Wealthy man, money is still the number one cause for murder. What else you got on him. No priors, married to Karen Steffens 45 who is a home realtor. They have a son Zack, all and all a normal family Lieutenant. Frank Steffens is a wealthy investor, whose building an outside mall Gambler; I don't think normal is part of his lifestyle. Alright we got a murdered investor who according to Doc. Lander was killed sometime this morning. The man was obviosity wealthy and as Keys pointed out money might be the cause. But before we jump to conclusions let's dot our I's and cross our T's. This man was an important figure, we need to solve this before the media blows it up. Monroe, Keys you take point and talk with the wife. Gambler you and Rakes dig into Frank's life, start with his finances. Copy that LT, let's go I'm driving. What...? You doing your thinking thing again. It's nothing Monroe. With you it's never nothing Keys, so spill it. I'm looking at Frank's file on his building and it looks like they were almost done with it. Looks like there were some holds on some of the other building permits that were being built in that plaza. Why would he put a hold on them? (Keys thinks intently) I don't know, it might be nothing, or it might be something. Didn't you say he was co-owner, who was the other guy? I don't know his name not in the file. Alright I hear you Keys, but hold on to that thought, where at the Steffens house. Let's break the news to the wife and go from there. On second thought since LT won't this wrapped up let's kill two birds with one stone. I want to run with this and head to the building job-site. You can talk with the wife and get her insights. I mean between the both of us you are better with words. I'm not trying to step on your toes or anything...No I like it and you're right I agree we can cut time in half if we divide and conquer. Alright keep your phone on you and we'll meet up later. Copy that. Fella's how we doing today...? Detective Hank Keys are you the foreman for this site? Yea that's me detective. Can I get a minute? You working hard out here sir, a lot of people can't wait for the opening? Yea, working on my last nerves, this plaza headed to its five yard-line of being completed. I got my guys in overtime trying finish and of course today be the day Frank doesn't show up. (Benson sighs) I'm sorry detective you said you wanted to talk, is everything ok? I can't say but speaking of Mr. Frank, what can you tell me about him? Can you give me a little back round on him? Is he in some kind of trouble or something detective? Or something…just answer the question for me. Uh yea Frank's a hard worker, we started flipping buildings right after college. Next thing we know we own a few dozen plaza's. I see… so you know him pretty well, almost grew up together? Not really, we were good friends our freshmen year in college. We both major in business management and decided to go into business together. You two doing very well for yourself, I can see. What else can you tell me? What's not too to say. Despite being extremely wealthy, unlike most people he was normal. How so? I mean if you saw him walking down the street, you would think he was just another average joe. You mean he wasn't too loud. I can say the same thing to you sir. (Benson smiles) Yea, I learned from him, if you walk around too loud you get too many eyes on you, and those eyes will stab you in the back in a heartbeat. But you have to admit, you two are building an outside mall I'm pretty sure people notice. Yea, but we always kept a low profile detective, like I said Frank wasn't like that… it's just the man he is. He shows up for work, do his thing, run the crew, and go home. (Benson sighs) I take it since you're here he must be in some kind of trouble, he's never late? What is his thing, I'm mean what does he do on these sites? Frank's the book guy he mostly handles the permits, licensees, payroll and all that, you know the business side. Everything else I take care. Every machines, vendors, and supervising the crew. So yesterday everything was good, was Frank acting strangely or anything? Strangely… no sir detective Frank was Frank just another day, he was finalizing a few other permits that was being stalled, but to my knowledge everything was good. Alright I appreciate your time I'll let you get back to it Mr….? Benson…Richard Benson. Is Frank ok detective? (Keys turn and stares) No he's not… Again thank you for your time and I'll be in touch. (ring ring) Doctor Lander you got something for me? Yea I measure the gunshot wound and base on the size it looks like you looking for a 22. At lease we know the type of gun were looking for. Did you ever figure out what made the other holes? Indeed, I did, I took a closer look at the wounds and base on my personal experience these wounds were made by a bolt gun. A bolt gun? Never heard of that? Probably wouldn't detective. I actually was shot by one in the leg when I was a kid. Learned the hard way, if you don't know how to use it right it will turn on you. Sorry to hear that doctor. Oh it's nothing detective, I was just a kid, it was an accident.

Well I'm glad you're ok doctor. Me too detective, but back to it, I spent more than half my life growing up on a farm, it's a type of gun my father and uncles use to slaughter the pigs humanly. Humanly...

so the pigs won't feel it when the gun was being used. Exactly right, that was the idea, the point of the gun was that animal felt nothing. (Keys intently thinks) Seems like the murderer had the same idea. Alright thanks Doc anything else? Yea is your partner with you? Uh no she and I went in different directions she's talking with the wife of the victim, Why? No reason I tried calling her but it went straight to voicemail, I guess she's busy. No worries I'm still processing the body so if I find anything else I give you a call. Alright thank you Doctor. (ring ring) Monroe…hey I'm leaving the construction site, talked to the partner and according to him Frank was a hard-worker despite being wealthy he was normal. Partner told me yesterday he was having a little trouble with a few permits, but all and all everything was good. I don't know he didn't really give me anything. How about you, how it go on your end with the wife? After I broke the news about her husband she broke down on me. After a while and she collected herself I gave her the normal questions. How was their relationship and all that and long story short they were a normal family. So no red flags there? They had their fights like everyone else, nothing ever violent, well according to her. Did you get the sense it was about his money? No I didn't get the gold digger vibe from her, I mean she said she and Frank was married before he made his money and even then they were a happy, stable family. Anyways I told her I'd be in touch if I had more questions, I thought it best to give her and her son time to grieve. She has to break the news to him after he gets home from school. Yea I hear you, so what's next? I told her as soon as her son gets home that they should come to the district just to be safe. Trying to make sure no one is targeting them, you know can't be too safe. (Monroe sighs) Let's see if Gambler and Rakes got something, let's meet-up at the district. Copy that. Back so soon, the wife didn't give you anything Monroe. Not really Rakes, she broke down on me which is to be expected. I gave her a few hours, she and her kid are going to come here afterward. I gave her my card if I don't hear anything, then I'll go and check with her and the kid. We came back to see what you two dug up. We did a deep dive on his finances and no red flags jumped out. The first thing we looked at was his will and yes once he is decease everything goes to his wife. Which would be the standard in all marrying millions couples. It happens all the time Monroe. She kills him take his money and run off with the pool guy. You watch way too many movies Gambler. The truth hurt, but this will was written by Frank years ago right around when he first started making his money. Which also means that if the wife wanted his money she would have done it years ago. Not necessarily Rakes, I mean the longer he's alive the more he makes, she could have been biting her time to get the most she can out of him. It's a stretch, but patients is a virtue. I'm not so sure guys I just talk to her and I didn't pick up those vibes. Your vibes might be right Monroe, seems like Mr. Frank had a bit of trust issues. How so Rakes?

According to the contract he and his lawyer made, upon his death all his assets goes into a trust fund for his son. Does his wife know about this?

I don't know you'll have to ask her, but she doesn't have access to it.

The kid will have access to it on his eighteen birthday, other than that the lawyer gives him a sort of allowance every now and then. So we still thinking money the motive and the wife or lawyer is the suspect. I don't know, what do you want us to do LT? (Lieutenant grinds and sighs) I want you and Keys to head back to the Steffens house. So your money is on the wife too, well it's been a few hours, she might have calm down I can take my run at her again. That won't be necessary, I just got a call…Karan Steffens has been murdered. (Everyone stares with silence) I thought you said she was inconsolable not suicidal Monroe! So this is my fault…you blaming me Gamble! Monroe, Keys to the

Steffens house now! Gamble, Rakes talk to this lawyer I want to know everything about these contracts and will. As I said earlier I want this solved quickly and quietly. Yes, sir. Copy that LT. Some tension between you and Gamble. You gone start on me Keys, you saying it's my fault too? I'm not saying anything; no one can really predict what's going to happen after they hear a loved one has passed. (Monroe sighs angrily) Yea, I should have seen it though Keys, she was a wreak after I told her. After I left her she said she was getting some air, headed to the park to feed the ducks. Feed the ducks? Yea, you know how the old people do, they feed the ducks and pigeons, don't judge so much it's actually quite relaxing. Plus, everyone grieves in their own way. Some yell their lungs out, some blame God, while other do something to keep their mind clear... like revenge. (Keys shows confusions) Ok!? But back to feeding ducks, that's something, I might give it a try one day. Yea you should… here we are. Patrolmen you first on scene? Patrolmen? You real funny Monroe. My apologies…detective Steven…I see you, what can you tell us? (Stevens cracks a smile) Smartass…I was in the area responding to a robbery at this address, came over and discovered the body, closed off the scene until you got here. Robbery? Who called it in? Unknown caller. Yea I know, trace the call to a phone booth about two blocks from here. You know I think New York is the only state to still use phone booths. You might be right about that Stevens. What the caller say? Voice just said and I quote, I think I hear gunshots and windows being broken. (Monroe stares with confusions) I was just here a few hours ago with her. Was anything taken? Didn't get around to process the house yet, as I said I was waiting on you two. Door wasn't tampered with, but two windows are broken. Alright Stevens, how about we take the body and you take the house. Your Hank Keys right? That's right. Monroe you good with this? (Keys smiles with pettiness) Why wouldn't she be...something on your mind Stevens? You said you was here before? I mean you two were the last people the victim spoke to before she died. Actually Stevens...no wait partner yea, we were the last people she spoke to, did you need to ask us some questions? Not yet I still got to process the scene, but don't worry you'll be the first to know something...excuse me. (Keys scoffs) I'm sure I will. Why did you do that keys we both know she only talk to me? Am I talking to myself? (Monroe sighs with annoyance)

You're doing your thinking thing again aren't you? Several holes to the back of the head and look at this one, powder burns were she was shot. Alright…first Frank and now his wife, you think they were targeted Keys? Maybe, take a closer look around Monroe… notice anything missing. There's no blood anywhere…no splatter, no blood pool, nothing. Yea, this a secondary too, which mean just like Frank she was killed somewhere else. There's also another similarity here, just like the first crime scene I believe the killer planned it. Really what make you say that keys? I'm not sure yet still putting the pieces together. How you holding up you ok Monroe? (Monroe sighs with grieve) Yea, I mean I'm good, like I said I was with her not to long ago. To be honest I'm kind of relieved it wasn't a suicide, but still she was a sweet woman she didn't deserve that.

You said she wanted to clear her head right? You know what park she went to? Well she was walking down the street when I was driving away. So? So detective Keys, the only park within walking distance of her house is Rosemary Park. And If I'm not mistaking that park has a beautiful pond full of ducks. You think she was killed there and then brought here Keys. Again I'm just thinking out loud but 3rd and Maple is a high jogging and workout area where we found Frank's body. Now Rosemary Park another high traffic area. But Karen's body is right here in her home Keys. Right, but this is the secondary I'm betting we find something at that park. (Monroe jokingly laughs) Look at you being all perspective… in that case I'll call Gamble and Rakes to close off that park, until we get there so we don't lose any evidents. Doctor Lander is five minutes out; she can tell us more. Only thing we know they were shot, so what do you think made the others holes Keys? A bolt gun…yea, I know I didn't get around to mention it, but Lander, upon examining Frank's body, said it was a bolt gun. You just now telling me this now Keys, some partner. She said she tried calling you earlier, but you didn't answer. I didn't get a call. I told her you were busy with the widow, but that's all she had was the weapon and that she thinks it was a 22 that was the kill shot. I see...first it's the husband now his wife, let's get the kid out of school and put him in protective custody. After that we'll meet up with Gamble and Rakes at the park. You don't won't to wait for the Doctor Monroe? Hey Stevens, doctor Lander is on her way, you got this here. Hilarious…Yea I got this I'll be in touch detectives.

{**NARRATIVE**: Their several sayings; when you sneeze…means someone is talking about you, when one of your eyes start to twitch…means something about today is just not right. When all these, let's call them bad vibes, hit you at once it's irrelevant…because from the moment you woke up and took that first breath of the day… you knew.} LT just called they picked up the kid he's good at the station. That's good. Yea, I got him up to speed on the case and he agree about going to the park. So Rakes and Gamble on their way to the park? Yes, sir their going to meet us there. So to some things up, we're thinking Karen was killed in the park and then placed at her house. Frank was discovered at Maple and 3rd but we're thinking he was killed elsewhere and place there. Both with several holes to the back of the head, but only one of the holes was a gunshot wound. And to add it up, you're saying the killer wanted the bodies to be found. Basically some's it up Keys? Something like that, only I think the killer made a mistake. How so? Everybody makes mistake Monroe, I'm not sure yet, I'll know more if we find something at the park. That doesn't make any sense Keys, you obviously have a theory. Yea, only if we find something, but we may not find anything, so a theory is just what it is, a theory.

(Monroe sighs with confusions) You know sometimes your thing that you do is really annoying, but I get it. Can you at least give me something to go on, I mean once we get to the park what do you think we should be focus on looking for? (Keys side stares) In my opinion…blood…a lot of it. Hey you mind telling us what where doing here Monroe? Yea we closed off the park soon as LT called. Hey to you too detective Gamble and Rakes. I tell you just rude... alright we're here because we think that Karan Steffen was killed here at the park and then placed at her house. What make you think that? After I spoke to her about her husband's death she told me she was headed to this park. She said feeding the ducks was relaxing and her stress reliever.

Really? (Keys chuckles) I know right, I said the same thing Rakes.

(Monroe annoyingly stares) Anyways, few hours later she was dead in her home, but we believe she was killed here first then placed at her home. This a big park Monroe. I can see that Gamble, which is why you two are here. (Gamble scoffs) Of course. Alright so what are we looking for? Gun or blood? Be on the lookout for both Rakes. Gun? Yea, sorry didn't get a chance to update you two on what the doctor said. Both Frank and Karen were shot execution style. She thinks it was a 22 maybe. Then what's the deal with the extra holes in the head? We think it was a smokescreen or the killer was planning on dumping the bodies in the river. Holes in the head you sink faster. Yea I'm not sure about dumping the bodies in the river part Monroe. I think the extra holes in the heads were for the killer pleasure. Or maybe overkill. Yea you may be right Rakes. Interesting you would agree with that Keys. Not now Gamble. No he's right it's just a profile, I overthink a lot. We'll you got my interest keys, why you think it gave him pleasure? I'm not sure yet as I was telling her it depends if we find something here. And if we don't?

Then where back at square one. Alright if we're all caught up here, let's split up to cover more ground. I called and got two more guys to help with the search. Who we get Monroe? Rodgers and Hobbit. Rodgers huh…Yea I made a call to Rodgers and LT sent in Hobbit. Gamble you're with me and Rodgers, we'll take the north end. Keys you Rakes and Hobbit take the south end, and we'll meet up in the middle, keep your phone's on. Copy that. (Gang splits up) So how you like it Keys? Like what? The switch from missing person to homicide. (Keys scoffs) You too Rakes, if you got something to say then say it? Just making small talk, and just for the record I don't judge people on their past. It's not my past I'm getting my judgment on Rakes…It's my generation. Isn't that one of the main reasons you became a cop? It's just one of those things in this world we get. I mean you hear it all the time, there are 1 and 5 chances of this or 1 and million chances of that. Somebody has to be the 1 and it's just so happen I'm the 1. You don't really think that? Yea, my mother gave birth to a tragedy, guess I'm just trying to wash some of the blood of my generations hands. (Rakes scoffs) Your generation doesn't have anything to do with you Keys. It's what you do and the choices you make that defy you. And for what it's worth, despite of what everyone else think of you, I got your back. Preciate that Rakes. What are we appreciating!? Damn Hobbit why you sneaking around? (Hobbit laughs) Well I didn't won't to interrupt your little moment you two were having there. It was beautiful by the way. Did you find anything, while you were all in our conversation Hobbit? Monroe said we was looking for a gun in this huge Park, I looked all around didn't find one, no surprise there. (Hobbit sighs with anger) This whole search might be a huge waste, I mean it's been what almost two days since both the Steffens were murdered, and we thinking we going to just stumble upon the gun? You said it yourself Keys Rosemary Park is well known for its high traffic of people. I mean how do we know someone didn't pick it up, or threw it in the river or something? (Rakes asks with annoyance) Are you done Hobbit, that's what we're here for to check and plus you weren't doing anything at the district anyways just pushing paper, might as well enjoy this beautiful weather and help us look. Anytime I can get some overtime I guess I can't complain. Just wish we know where in this vast park to look. Hold on didn't Monroe say that Karen like to feed the ducks Keys? Did she say ducks? Yea Hobbit, I had the same reaction apparently its relaxing and it's on my list to do. No time like the present… let's check by the pond. Good call. (ring ring) hold on… Rakes… Alright I'll tell them. Hey, Gamble said they got something. It's about time… where are they? (Rakes sighs with surprise) By the pond… looks like they beat us to it, alright where on the way. What's wrong with you Keys? What nothing. Hey you must have been thinking what we was, you beat us here… what we got Monroe? Found this in the sewer drain. What is that… a silencer? (Monroe stares intently) Yea, I figure the killer tried to toss it in the pond…, it looks like the drain bars caught it before the water carry it away. And look at this, look like a blood smear on the bench. Someone tried to clean up. Guess your instincts were right Keys. (Gamble scoffs) I'm sure it was. Gamble did you say something? I was just saying it's going to be a long shot in finding anything on this Monroe. The water most likely destroyed any blood and prints. It doesn't matter this is now a crime scene. Rodgers call this in and roll in the crime unit. Copy that. Well wait Monroe, again not trying step on your toes, but we don't know if the blood is Karen? (Keys stares with focus) Assuming our theory is correct so far, we know that Frank Steffen was murdered early yesterday morning with several holes to the back of the head, but the kill shot was a 22. Few hours later, we saying we believe Karen Steffen was killed here and then moved to her house...same kill type.

(Monroe agreeably sighs) Yea, you got a point Keys, we need to compare this blood and if it come back positive then we got our primary for Karen murder. (Gamble scoffs with anger) Well look at you two… ok if this our primary for Karen, why moved her to her house, I mean Rosemary Park is another high traffic area, someone would have spotted the body eventually, just like Frank. Maybe the killer didn't won't the body to be found that way this time. Yea maybe. (Monroe sighs) Well until then we're going to run with this theory and see where it goes. Gamble you and Hobbit head back to the district and put a rush on that blood, I won't to know who it is. Copy that. In the meantime, Keys you and Rakes go back to 3rd and maple. What for? We know Frank wasn't killed there, but moved there. Maybe he was killed somewhere near 3rd and

Maple. If our theory is right then Karen was killed here and then moved to her home, a few blocks away. Frank was found at 3rd and maple. (Rakes understandably sighs) Then we thinking he was killed blocks away, yea I got you Monroe. I have done this before thank you. (Monroe smiles) Just making sure we all caught up rookie… I mean Rakes. Rodgers if you want to make some overtime you can do a final sweep of the park just in case we missed something. Plus, if that blood come back as Karen then I'll need you here to close the scene. Love it when you take charge like that Monroe. What about you? I'm going to head back to the Steffens house and see if our friend detective Stevens got something. I'm pretty sure he's waiting to spring something up. (gang splits up again) It's a nice day for a walk Keys. What was that? Just trying make small talk while were walking. Is there something on your mind Rakes? (Rakes smiles) Alright you got me, it's this case, is it just me or does this seem like this is too easy? (Keys smiles) No it's not just you, I can't shake this feeling myself. Right…so I'm not crazy Keys? No you're not crazy. Crazy is what I get every day. (Rakes stares creepily at Keys) You know I've been detective for going on 8 years now and to this day I still can't get a read on you Keys. I guess I'm doing something right then Rakes. I mean though all the criticism and hateful stares people give you, how are you always so calm? What you go through on a day and day has to take a toll, not to mention you're a detective. I don't know if I could do it. (Keys sighs with pride) What can I say I just block out everyone else's noise towards me. It's easier to focus on the present and it's makes everything quite, I like the quite. (Rakes eyes open with confusion) Ok...? I don't think you know the definition of small talk, that was kind of deep. (Keys smiles) It's a beautiful day. (Rakes smiles) That was better and yes It is, so we are looking for blood somewhere near here? I mean walking around looking for blood splatter doesn't necessary mean it belongs to Frank. People run and workout over here daily, there's bound to be blood and sweat everywhere. Yea exactly Rakes, if someone wanted to commit a murder, why not choose a high traffic area... I would. (Rakes side looks) Really? Don't start with me Rakes it's just a metaphor. That's not what I meant, I just had an idea, but It might be a little weird for you Keys. After a day like today I can use a little weird. What you got? (Rakes cracks a smile) I was thinking what would you do? Excuse me…? I mean if you just killed Frank, where would you do it? Hmmm... See I told you it would be weird. I guess someone like me would know a little something about murder. That's not what I'm saying Keys I'm just thinking outside the box here. (Keys cracks a smile) No it's fine I like it, alright let me see. Well in any murder, I always ask myself the basic five questions…For me anyways. Who, what, where, when, and how. When applying to this case we have the when; according to Dr. Lander Frank was killed yesterday morning around 6 and then his wife Karen a few hours later around 2 in the afternoon. The how; we know bliss attack from behind, several holes to the back of the head follow by a gunshot which we thinking was the kill shot. You don't think it was Keys? No I don't…My original thought was that the holes was a smokescreen to cover up the gunshot. Now I'm thinking it's the other way around. Why is that? The weapon that made the holes in both victims. A bolt gun…A bolt gun? Yea I didn't know what it was either, but according to Lander, it's a type of gun used to kill pigs and cows humanly. (Rakes shows confusion) I'm not following. The gun is design so that animal doesn't feel anything. So you're saying the killer shot them in the back of the head with the bolt gun killing them instantly and then shot them several more times and afterward shot them with the gun to make us believe that the gun was the original kill shot. I don't know Keys sounds like a big stretch. It's what I would do…I mean you asked me what I would do If I killed him. Alright alright so you were saying. We got the when and the how…I suppose the who;

would be Frank and Karan Steffen right? Correct…so far the Steffens are our who and that's our biggest problem. How so? Well so far we got only two murders but if someone else gets killed by the same murder then we have to keep going back to the five questions and it gets frustrating. So for now it's our job to keep the who to a minimum, preferable one…or even better none. (Rakes sighs and agree) The day I wake up and there is no more murder or nobody is killing each other; that's the day hell freezes over. That's what we're here for Rakes, to keep some balance. How about the what and where? We're at our where…Frank was found here at 3rd and maple and Karen we believe she was killed at Rosemary Park. Both killed in high traffic areas, which brings us back to the why. My thoughts were that the killer or killers wanted the bodies to be found. Again why…I don't know yet maybe a challenge to the police, maybe it's about their money a simple vendetta, or just maybe he or she is a psychopath who gets off on the kill. Ok that's a little deep Keys. Well it's true, you've seen it yourself some of the people you've put away. Some of those families' kill just because they can or it's in their blood, they like it, no remorse…just for the thrill. (Rakes stares at Keys) You mean those people kill. Yea, that's what I said Rakes. Ok all that leave is the what. Well what can be a strong word. The what in this case for me would be what kind of person would do this. What did Frank and Karen Steffen do to deserve this type of butchery. (Keys looks with focus) The biggest what for me is if I committed these murders…what will I do next and why do I get the feeling like this has something to do with me. You...what are you saying you think someone's after you? I don't know Rakes, but I can't shake the feeling that I've seen this before. Seen what? (Rakes sighs with confusion) Ok ok before you get all paranoid on me, let's focus on the here and now.

Now what would you do if this was you? You just killed Frank and laced him near 3rd and Maple, now where did you do it? Somewhere secluded, and I'll have to be quick because we acknowledge that this was a high traffic jog area. Assuming he was jogging I would sneak up from behind, shoot him with the bolt gun and drag his body to a secluded area...Like in that ally Keys? Exactly... not too in your face noticeable and plenty of places for solitude. Let's look around and see if we can find anything.

(Rakes walks down ally) Hey I got something. Look right here, looks like blood on the drainpipe. Alright let's get a sample and put a rush on it. Looks like you were right Keys, if this blood is a match for Franks then we just found where he was murdered. (Keys scoffs) Yea, and if I am right… things about to get worse Rakes. You thinking another murder? I'm thinking I need to do what I do in all my cases I get. Which is? My favorite president quote. Ok you lost me, where are you going with this? (Keys smiles) Lincoln and he's famous for always saying; whatever you do in life always have a contingency. Is that so? Yea maybe it's just a feeling but me being who I am, you can't be too careful. (Rakes sighs and agrees) Ok!? Yea, maybe I can help you with that. (ring ring) Keys…Yea, ok we'll be right there. That was the LT, they need us back at the district.

{**NARRATIVE**: I like mysteries…when you solve them it's sort of a rush, a good feeling at outsmarting the killer at his own game. You might not want to admitted it but, defeating a worthy challenge or challenger it's intoxicating. Deep down you know I'm right. I suppose your telling yourself I know what's going to happen here, I've seen this 1000 times before. Exactly… and that notion right there is why Fate always throws a curve ball, rather we seen it coming…or it already hit you in your face}. Hey Keys and I may have found Frank's primary kill site. Yea we found blood a few blocks down an ally on a drainpipe. Can you run this for me Hobbit and if it comes back as a match for Frank then our theory will hold. (Rakes looks with confusion) Who is that with the LT? Who you think Rakes… Internal Affairs. What the hell Internal Affairs doing here? (Keys scoffs) Let me guess Monroe…Styles? Yea it's him Hank. Of course it is, so what now? (Rakes stares) I take it you and he have history? If only you knew Rakes. (Monroe stares at Keys) The blood on the park bench was a match to Karen. So she was killed there? Well her blood was there, but so far it's looking like it. (Keys looks confuse) So what's the problem? (Monroe sighs) The silencer. What about it? You remember that raid we were in few years back Keys? Ugh, yea Noah Bennet, as I recall he was sex trafficking over 17 girls, one of them in whom we were looking for. How can I forget that raid was one of our first shootout. O yea I remember that. Yea we found the girl and a warehouse full of guns. So what you saying the silencer that was found was part of that gun stacks? Yes, but that's not the problem Keys. When taking inventory, a number of guns and silencers were missing. I remember, and I also remember that we were cleared of that accusation. Yes, we were, but that silencer that we found at the park, turns out to be one of the silencers that went missing. We process and dusted it and...your print was on it. (Keys pause and stares) So what are you saying Monroe? Calm down I'm not saying anything, I'm just telling you what I just got grilled for. Giving you a heads up, we were the primary on that raid, so it's not a shock their looking at us. (Keys scoffs and smiles) You mean me, don't worry about it it's nothing new, use to it. Keys can you join us in here please!? While you wasting time being grilled,

Hobbit, Rakes, and I are going to join Gamble and check this other blood. (Keys walks in room) Lieutenant… Mr. Styles can't say I'm surprise to see you. The feelings mutual detective but I'm not here to reminisce in the past. (Keys cracks a smile) I know why you're here, I suppose you going to ask me did I do these murders, you know the usual dance between us. I take it your partner told you about the print? Yes, she did and of course my prints are on it, as well as the other guns we seize, I was there. Can we move this alone I got a case to get back to. You know the drill Keys just let I.A ask their questions and we can move on. Fire away. That raid you and Monroe were in was the warehouse of a Mr. Noah bennet correct? That's what the file says. He was a low-life scum who sex-traffic teenage girls. Other than girls he traded drugs, money, and of course guns. You got me all wrong detective it was a good raid. Then why am I here, I told you I don't have time to do our little dance. I'm getting to it…you also had an incident, according to you, a few hours after that raid. There it is… yes I lost my gun but I did the paperwork and notify the lieutenant as I'm sure he can attest to that. (Styles smiles) You mean this gun…, is this your gun detective? Can't tell, no worries let me put it under the light so you can get a better look. (Styles smiles again) Wait, want to see a little trick, you see that silencer, with your print on it by the way, it just so happens that this silencer and this gun are a perfect match. (Keys just stares) Look at that some trick, but can't say I'm surprise. No I suppose you wouldn't be; I mean I guess you would be used to it. Is there a question Styles? Yes, lieutenant I'm still waiting on my answer. Detective is this your gun? No it's not, but I get the feeling you already knew that. (Styles side smiles) Hmmm that thing you always do you know it's irritating sometimes. So I have been told. Lieutenant can you give us the room, me and detective Keys here have to get better acquainted. I'll go check with the others on that blood. Keys when you're done wasting time with Mr. Styles meet us back in the lab. Copy that LT. (LT leaves) Now can we cut to the chase? I know why this isn't my gun, how do you? It's not that hard to figure out detective. You know every time there is a cop shooting Internal affairs is involved. I know. Well, if you know then who do you think did the paper work on that raid you and your partner was in? (Keys turns away) Excuse me if I'm not surprise, you've been circling me ever since I became a detective.

Nothing personal detective just doing my job. Let's agree to disagree, now I'm still waiting on my answer. Of course, well as you know a number of guns and silencers were uncounted for after taking inventory. Me and my partner were cleared of any and all accusations, as I recall it was you who cleared us. Your right but whoever said the case was closed. I just cleared you two. I see. No you don't see, not yet. (Styles circles Keys) After I cleared you two I go through your report. In their it mentions you lost your gun. I know as I said before, I was there. Your gun is a standard police issue firearm. In your report you stated you customize it with your LT approval. Well after a lot of searching around I found the artist that did the job. (Keys grins) There it is, and that's how you figured out this wasn't my gun. You tried to match the symbol on this gun and it wasn't a match. Your half right detective, your partner and your LT and everyone all knew about this symbol. So when this gun was found and this silencer with your print on it, well that should be case close. And then you add that whole thing with your history. (Keys sighs with irritation) Your wasting my time Mr. Styles. I'm getting to it detective. Get to it faster. This being a small town there are only a handful of artist that can do such a good job. I mean putting a dragon on here, that takes special skills. Do you want his number or something? That won't be necessary Keys, I already had a conversation with him. It seems like you paid for a little something extra to be added to this symbol. Guess I should have paid a little more for his discreet. Don't worry after learning what it was and how it works I choose to keep that information to myself. So when you asked if this was my gun it was some sort of a test. Something like that. Only two people knew about that symbol, the artist and myself, and now you make three Mr. Styles. This gun was used to kill Mr. and Mrs. Steffen and with the blood and your prints on the silencer, everything points to you. Sounds like you have some reservation, that's not like you Mr. Styles. Don't be a wise ass Keys, as you said earlier we got history and these murders doesn't scream Hank Keys to me. You think you know me? (Styles smiles with envy) Just enough to know you didn't do these murders. Back to this gun and to answer your question, after my conversation with the artist and after processing this gun with a fine tooth comb. That's when I noticed it, the symbol that will only show up under intense light. A beautiful yin-yang symbol in the middle of the dragon. That's how I knew this wasn't your gun. (Keys smiles) So when you shine that light on this gun earlier, I take it that was a show for my LT? Someone is going out their way to frame you detective. That's nothing new, but that raid was almost 15years ago. I Know just like you I was there too, which tells me this was well planned out. I mean 15years, now that's dedication. I'm somewhat envious. Can't say I'm surprised, with me it's always something. After all these years you still a strange one Keys. So where do go from here Styles? You still got a case to solve, as far I'm concern It's still an open investigation. What about the gun? Inconclusive, as I said still an ongoing case. If that's all excuse me then, got a case to get back to. (Style turn and grins) Detective!! Even the best of us need a little help, that pride of yours might be the death of you someday. So you helping me now Styles? Just some advice, and shouldn't have to tell you but let's keep our little conversation between us. Have a good day detective Keys, I'll be in touch. (Keys scoffs and smiles) Hmmm wouldn't expect nothing less Mr. Styles…see you around. You alright Keys? Nothing new partner, just another day, what we got on the blood? It came back positive for Karen. Afraid of that, but so far our theory is holding, so now we know she was killed at that bench and then placed at her house. What about the blood Rakes and I found? Yes, sir positive for Frank. Same signature killed by the dumpster and placed on 3rd and Mable. (Gamble scoffs angrily) So we all just going to ignore the elephant in the room? Did I miss something Gamble?

Lieutenant are you still allowing him in this investigation? Him? Whose him? Gamble if you got something to say then say it I'm standing right here. (Gamble walks towards Keys) Ok, why is your print on the silencer that killed Karen Steffen? I.A had you in there a pretty long time? Really Gamble, I.A had me in there just as long, are you going to accuse me too? No not you Monroe just your partner. You're getting really out of line Gamble we all cops here. Don't give me that Rakes, I'm just saying what were all been thinking. Still judging me on my family's history I see. (Keys squares up to Gamble) You know Gamble I could take this knife right now slit your throat and polish my shoes with your blood still dipping I could do that, but I'm nothing like my family. And as to answer your earlier question, if memory serves it was you who said that the water most likely destroyed any prints and blood? Also wasn't it you who processed the silencer… and shocker my prints just happen to be on it. Just what the hell are you saying keys!! Doesn't feel good to always be the suspect does it Gamble? Alright that's enough everyone take a breath! Gamble you said your piece, but Rakes was right your way out of line. Keys a good detective and we don't judge a man for his or her past. We all got past even me. Now we know no one in this room committed these murders which means the killer is still out there. I told you all once before I wanted this solve before it got out to the public. So how about we start acting like detectives, am I clear? Copy that Lt. Copy that. So what's next? It looks like your theory is starting to become reality. So do we have any suspects? Monroe? We were looking at the wife but that ship has sailed when she was murdered LT. What about you two, Gamble, Rakes... you got anyone in mind? No sir, our money was on the wife as well. Keys, what about you? Other than the wife there's Franks partner. A Mr. Richard Benson, he and Frank building that plaza downtown. According to him he and Frank was good friends and partners for years. Doesn't make sense. Well money is still the number one motive for killing. I don't know LT, seems too easy. (LT sighs with confusions) Be that as is may, why don't you take another run at him. Monroe I want you to head back to the Steffens house, detective Stevens is asking for you, seems he found something. Rakes you and Gamble visit doctor Lander, by now she should have finished her autopsy. Copy that. And Gamble...your opinions are noted but keep them to yourself. Copy LT. (Monroe grins) You're doing your thinking thing again. Can you blame me Monroe, did you hear the LT; your opinions are noted. I know Keys but we got a job to do. I'll head to the Steffens house and you get back to the partner and we'll go from there. Yea I hear you I'll catch up with you later.

[**NARRATIVE**: Trust... It can be a dangerous weapon to the vulnerable and desperate. I mean we see it every day don't we? Even down to a simple gesture as to can I buy you a drink? You ask yourself did he put something in my drink? Up to a bigger gesture as to you can trust me, I'll help you… You never know... It is often sometimes said that when you live with or worked with someone for years you start to gain their trust. It is also said trust no one...

Not even family. Those two statements are in their own, absolute correct. Question is, when in a dangerous situation as to being a cop, or any profession, which should you heed more, or better yet why not both?] Looks like you're on the five-yard line with this plaza Mr. Benson.

Detective Keys…never good news if your back here again. Last time we spoke you said Frank wasn't ok? (Benson sighs) I haven't seen or heard from him in days so I can only assume. Your assumption would be correct Mr. Benson. Frank was murdered. For someone claiming to be his best friend you don't seem too broken up. Don't read so much into it detective, like you I don't wear my emotions on my sleeves. Like me? Yea, I picked up on your vibe as soon as we first spoke. Don't worry it's a compliment.

Not even a smile detective? It's been a long day Benson, not in a smiling mood. I see, well if you thinking I killed Frank then you're wasting your time. I know. You know I didn't kill Frank or you know you're wasting time? I'm still debating that. Let me ask you something Benson, where do you keep your construction equipment? In a locked storage why? Can you show me please? Here it is detective. I assume you and Frank are the only ones with a key? You would be correct sir. Is there a piece of equipment you're looking for detective I can help? You are helping, is this your catalog for everything? Yes, sir I catalog every piece of equipment here. Mind if I take a look Benson? (Benson pause with confusion) Be my guess. As I said before detective I'm the last person to want Frank dead, he was my friend. What about his wife? Karen,

If you thinking she had anything to do with Franks death you're way off. Were in an agreement with that Mr. Benson. Yea, if that's all detective I have a funeral to plan. One more question, do you use bolt guns or any type of gun like that here? As a matter of fact, yes we do, but as you can see their all accounted for in the catalog. I need to take these for processing and then I'll get out of your hair, unless that's a problem. No sir, no problem at all, I won't justice for my friend. Good to know, well I'll let you get to your funeral planning, stay in town I'll be in touch Mr. Benson. I'm not going anywhere; by the way detective I think you got a shadow. (Keys cracks smiles) Yea, I know. (Keys starts walking) As you know I worked in narcotics then switch to missing persons. From time to time I had to go undercover and surprisingly I was really good at it.

Being able to get close to a person without them knowing takes a real certain type of art. Lord knows I'm not bragging it's just a state of fact, some people have that something and some people don't. (Keys side stares) And you...Rakes...are not one of those people, so are you just going to stand there? (Rakes sighs with embarrassment) Just so you know this wasn't my idea Keys, LT orders. To be honest I'm not surprise, especially after that spat me and Gamble got into earlier. (Rakes looks confuse) To this day I still can't get a read on you Keys. I don't know whether to be impressed or annoyed. I'll take that as a compliment Rakes. I'm serious Keys, despite everything and all the judgement you get on a regular base, you still keep this calm and collected vibe. Even now you already know everyone thinks you're a killer and you knew I was following you. And yet here you are not even the least bit phased. How do you do it? (Keys smiles) Good question, I guess it's just part of that annoying thing I'm told I do. (ring ring), yea go for Keys. Ok on my way, you staying or coming, got to meet Monroe at the Steffens house. (Rakes grins) You see that's exactly what I'm talking about Keys, that shit is really annoying. Sorry about that Rakes, you coming or going? (Rakes scoffs) I guess I'm coming, after all I'm supposed to be following you anyways, but how about we forget about that. Already forgotten Rakes. (Rakes and Keys enter house) Monroe, you found something you sounded hesitant on the phone? (Monroe stares with anticipation) Not me our friend detective Stevens found it. Rakes why are you here, I thought you and Gamble was with Doctor Lander? She still processing the wife's bodies, she was backed up with paper work, so LT sent me to back up Keys. (Keys looks around) Ok Detective Stevens are you going to tell me why I'm here? Well first good to see you too detective rudeness. Now as you recall, I was called here on a robbery call and upon arriving I found Karen Steffens body. Yea I know, can you get to it Stevens. (Steven gets annoyed) I'm getting to it now be quite. Anyways well as I'm pretty sure you know that this was staged as a robbery. Am I wrong? I figured that. Interesting you would say that Keys. Can you just show us what you found Stevens? Of course Monroe, crime scene found this under the floorboard. (Everyone just stares) What is that? It's a bolt gun Rakes. (Steven smiles) Exactly right detective Keys. A bloody bolt gun if you look closer and if memory serves wasn't it you who said that a bolt gun was the murder weapon? (Keys looks around) No just one of the murder weapons was a bolt gun. A 22 gun and a drill was used as well. And actually to clarify your statement, doctor Lander said the kill shot for both victims was a bolt gun, we believe the gunshot and the drill was just a smokescreen. A smoke-screen for what? That's what where trying to figure out. I am assuming you process the bolt gun Stevens? Something like that Monroe, I took a picture and sent it back to the district. My guy there is processed it and I'm waiting on the results now. (Keys scoffs) I see, you called me here to brag, so if my prints come back on the gun or something you will be the one to bring me in. Is that what you think of me Keys? I simply called you and your partner here to share information, after all don't we all won't the same thing? I sincerely doubt that Stevens. (Steven scoffs) Be that as it may the results should be here in a minute. Did you know about this little ambush Monroe? After all these years as your partner I'm going to ignore what you just asked me. But to ease your mind, after I showed up Stevens kept me in the dark. He wouldn't tell me anything until I called you. It's all good Monroe, Smartass Stevens and his so call evident is my last concern. Sticks and stones detective. There it is again; I swear that thing of yours is highly annoying. Really Monroe. Rakes you know what I meant. So what is it now Keys, what's wrong? Something not right. (Rakes sighs with confusion) Won't to elaborate that? We are standing in room where Mrs. Steffens body was found. I say that's not right at all. Are you talking about the bolt gun? Rakes, do you remember what you asked me when we were in the park? What you ask me to do? What? You mean what would you do if you were the killer? Excuse me? Don't worry about it Monroe it was just something we were acting out. In all case let's use that thinking here. There's no way in hell I would leave the murder weapon at the Steffens house. Your right Keys It's too smart, it's too easy. Exactly. Do you also remember the five question? Who, What, Where, When, and How? Yea, but I thought we answered them Keys? We did Rakes, but they can always be added on to. Your lost me Keys. Me too, just what are you getting at Keys. I'm getting there Monroe, It's almost like it's backward. What is? (Keys face sterns) Wrong place at the wrong time, but I'm thinking now where at the right place at the right time. What makes you say that Keys? I don't know yet

Monroe, why don't you tell me Stevens. (Monroe shows concern) What's wrong with you? Nothing Monroe, just trying join in on the conversation. No I mean what's wrong with you, you can't even stand up straight. Yea your sweating bullets you alright? So now you're concern with my health now Keys? (Monroe gasps with fear) He's right Stevens, your turning red and your nose is bleeding all over the place. (Stevens wobbles coughs repeatedly) What the hell Stevens! You threw up on me! What's wrong with you, you need a doctor!? (Stevens stops and collapse) Sorry about that Monroe…, guess I got a bug. (Monroe pause and gasps) Shit! Rakes call an ambulance; Keys give me your jacket I need to put it under his head. Hey! Hey! Stevens Stevens!!! You're going to be ok, just hang in there. (Stevens cracks a smile) Well I'll be damn, didn't see this coming. Don't talk like that Stevens ambulance is in rout. Oh God he's coughing up blood. Stevens!!! (Stevens stares blankly) Keys come here. You don't need to be talking Stevens, save your energy. For once, don't argue, just come here… (Stevens whisper) shadow. (Keys pause and hesitate) What you say!? Monroe where the hell is that ambulance? (Monroe starts to cry) It's New York Keys, still seven minutes out. Just keep hanging in there Stevens, you going to be ok. (Stevens smiles) Monroe… still optimistic as ever. Shut-up you idiot, I don't want to hear another word until that ambo is here. (Stevens last breath) Be... careful. (Monroe eyes widen) Stevens Stevens!!! Dear Lord he's dead. Everyone stand back and don't touch anything. Rakes cancel the ambulance and call this in and call Doctor Lander. Rakes? (Rakes face freezes) Oh my God. The way he died. Pull yourself together Rakes and call it in. (Monroe slaps Rakes) Rakes snap out of it!!! (Rakes gasps) Yea, I'm good I copy, this is detective Rakes we've gotten officer down, unknown cause, scene is secure, send crime scene and medical team now! (Monroe grins) That idiot Stevens might have been an ass, but he didn't deserve whatever that was happen to him. From what I saw and what we've seen before, I'm thinking poison. I'm pretty sure we can all agree on that Keys, but like I said don't touch anything and talk to no one until you're with your FOP. That diffidently goes to you too Keys. You don't have to remind me Monroe, I'm used to it remember and no I didn't kill him Rakes. Not funny, Stevens might have been an ass, but he was a good cop, I think we can all agree on that. Yea I suppose your right. (Monroe face intensify) By the way, before we get interrupted, what do you think he meant by be careful Keys? What? C'mon Hank we all heard what he said. Be careful, what do you think he meant by that? I don't know what you want me to say, I don't know. Why you looking at me like that? Is there something you want to say Monroe? Well he was looking at you Keys. Don't start with me again Rakes. She's right Keys. What the hell you want me to say, I got nothing I assume he was talking to all of us. (Monroe scoffs) I think before everyone gets here we all need to be on the same page. I know you two already know the drill but whatever questions we're asked just tell the truth. Why would any of us lie about what just happen Monroe? Rakes tell me what you see here?

What kind of question is that? O I see. See what Keys? Rakes the five questions remember. What about them. What are we doing here?

Monroe called you and said Stevens got something for us to see. The bloody bolt gun found under the floorboard. According to him he processed the gun and we're waiting on the results. Yea I know I still don't understand what I see. What Keys is trying to say Rakes is that we three showed up here because Stevens wanted to show us the bolt gun.

And as were waiting on the results to come back Stevens suddenly dies a horrible and tragic death. Do you see it now Rakes? You saying they going to think one of us killed him. Exactly. Don't look at me, it's just another Tuesday for me. So you saying one of us then Keys? Of courses not I'm just stating facts. Look we three was all standing right here when he collapsed, so like you said Monroe just tell them what we all saw and everything will be alright. I can hear the sirens, let's get this over with. (Monroe looks around) One more thing been nagging at me.

Can I ask you something Keys? What is it Kelly? What you said about it being backwards, wrong place at the wrong time but right place at the right time. What was that all about? Don't read too much into Monroe...call it intuition. One hell of an intuition Hank. Tell me about it.

(LT sighs with anger) Seems like my week just keep getting better.

Lieutenant. You want to know why my weeks keeps getting better? First I got my ass chewed out by the chief because somehow Franks and Karen's murder made the front page. Wait what!? No wait there's more, not only has this case becoming ten times more difficult, but apparently the chef suspects the leak came from us. Of course he does, You're not thinking one of us leak to the press? Of course not Monroe, I'm just telling you what I just got grilled for. And to sum up the week now we got yet another murder, a detective investigating our murder I might add. I knew Stevens, he was a good man, I don't know what the hell is going on but he didn't deserve this. What the hell you three standing around for, get to it, someone want to tell me what the hell happened? Yes, I'd like to know as well. (Keys scoffs) Styles… well that was quick. A cop was killed so yes

I.A is involve, you should know that and hello again to you too detective Keys. Let's skip the pleasantries why don't we, who wants to go first in explaining what happen here? My detectives aren't answering any questions Styles without their FOP presents. No need for the hostility Lieutenant just routine questions. It's fine Lieutenant we've got nothing to hide. Ok Monroe I'm all ears. (Monroe glares) I'll keep it simple for you Styles, I was informed by the LT that Stevens has discover something so he told me to meet up with him here. About a half hour later Stevens asked me to call detective Keys to come over to share information. Detective Keys and detective Rakes show up and Stevens began sharing information and evidents he discovered. I assume you are talking about this? What is that? It's a bolt gun LT, Stevens found it under the floor mat. So he found the murdered weapon for the Steffens? Yes sir, the initial murder weapon we discovered was a bolt gun. (Stevens sighs) I see, go on what happen next? After that Stevens informed us that he was waiting on a call from crime scene for the results. What results? There was blood smear on the gun, and he said he was able to lift a print. And… keep going? And after that we notices he was acting strange. Strange how? Well first he was wobbling like he couldn't stand up straight and then he started to sweat profusely. He started turning red and started having nose bleeds. He collapsed on the floor and I told Rakes to call an ambulance right away. Lastly he started coughing up blood and moments later, well here he is. As I have seniority, I instructed detective Rakes to call it in and informed both Rakes and Keys not to touch anything. Detective Rakes, Keys is all of what detective Monroe stated accurate? Every last word agent Styles. Well as you know I.A will launch an investigation so you all know the drill, I'll be in touch. What now Lieutenant? Just a few more years and I retire from this. This has already spiraling out of control, we got three murders and no suspects. Not to mention we still don't even know if their related. I'll tell you what we're going to do next. You three are going to go back to the district and write up your reports and turn them into I.A. What we don't need is I.A poking around and stalling this investigation. LT we've been at it for nearly 32 hours, we're running on fumes now. (LT stares with anger) Look at my face Monroe, does it look like I give a shit. You think you're running on fumes, I still have to make a statement to the press and not to mention the chef is still up my ass. As I told all of you from the start I wanted this wrapped up quickly and quietly, but looks like we're way passed that now aren't we. Sorry Lieutenant. I don't won't your apology, I want this put to bed. (LT sighs) Everyone go home...take a couple hours and afterwards get back to it, I want this solve before the weeks out understood? Yes, sir. Keys before you go I won't you to head back to the district and write up your report and go ahead and turn that in for me. Is there a reason for that Lieutenant? No reason at all detective, just I.A prefers your report while it's still fresh in your head. Is that a problem? No sir not a problem at all. Good I'll see you all in the A.M. (LT walks out) Well haven't seen LT like that in a while. You alright Keys? Me yea I'm good. Well that was really convincing but you want to try that again, mind as well share with the group. What!? Don't what me, It's obviously you have something on your mind. She's right Keys your starting to become predictable. Seems like I'm losing my touch, but really It's nothing lady's just tired. As a matter of fact, we're all tired so let's just do what LT told us and you two get some rest. I'll take of this paperwork and catch you all in the morning.

{**NARRATIVE**: It's tiring sometimes..., no let me change that..., it's downright exhausting all the time. Being judge as soon as you walk in a room for no reason, especially if you have... let's say an interesting past. Every last one of us I know can relate to this in some sort of way. Prime example; your first day at work or school you walk in and instantly you're automatically the target of someone's judgement.

Doesn't matter the reason; jealousy, envious, revenge, there are millions of reasons, but those three are usual the prime reasons. Some people will do everything in their power to see you fail to stroke their ego or keep their pride in tack. To me I guess that's why God created red flags. When you're prejudged automatically for whatever reason, certain red flags can be your life-line or just maybe your death warrant... like I said exhausting}. I thought I'd be the only here this late.

Hey what you doing here Keys? Gamble...I can ask you the same thing.

Well as you recall I was with Doctor Lander in the atopy room. She just finished up with the wife. And? And as we conclude, she was killed the same way as the husband. Blest attack from behind with the bolt gun and then shot. By the way I heard what happened to detective Stevens, it's a damn shame... he was a good man and father. You were there at the house with him, wasn't you Keys? You don't have to beat around the bush with me Gamble, you never have, so if you got something you want to ask me then ask. I thought I just did. Yea I was there along with Monroe and Rakes. Stevens discover some evidence and wanted to share with the group. The group huh? Yea, as I said Monroe and Rakes was there as well, so they plus me would be called a group. Your too funny Keys. Well I try not to be but base on the intent of your question it sounded like you needed a little clarity. Don't mistake me for I.A just trying to join in on the group is all. Then by all means ask away Gamble.

You said Stevens discover some evidence at the Steffens house right?

That's right. May I ask what this particular piece of evidents was? (Keys side smiles) You may ask, but something tells me you already know, so can we just end this little dance of ours and get to the point. Are you going to tell me the results or what Gamble, it's been a long and stressful week and I'm exhausted. (Gamble laughs hard) Hot damn you Keys!! You are one hell of a pain in my ass. You got to give me something Keys, how do you do it? Do what? That! That right there, that calm, serene vibe of yours. (Gamble sighs with envy) From a B cop in blue to a detective in missing person, and now homicide. Every case you've work you seem to be always two steps ahead of everyone. What you think we didn't notice. As soon as you get to a crime scene or even step into a room, the way you overanalyze everything by splitting it up and putting it back together again perfectly…fucking art. It's called being a detective Gamble, that's' what we do. No, that's what you do Keys… the rest of us are nowhere near you and the irony is deep down you know that. (Gamble stares up and sighs) I'm man enough to say I'm envious towards you Keys. That thing you always do is fucking annoying, but somehow it only works for you. It's really funny because we all tried it ourselves and not a damn one of us came remotely close to pulling it off. Hell even LT couldn't do it and that's saying something. I have to tip my hat to you detective Keys and say with respect, you are unique. What...? Nothing to say Keys? No witty comeback? No smartass remarks? You got nothing for me? (Keys blankly stares) Got nothing to say Gamble. I haven't the slightest clue as to what you've been talking about. Now as to, what I'm taking as a compliment of what you said as to me being unique, I will say to you I appreciate that. Now if it was your intent in belittling me to satisfy your ego then you can take your compliment and tip your hat and your ass out my face before I lose what little integrity I have left...with respect of course. (Gamble smiles) No sir detective I've no need for you to lose your integrity, we both know what you're capable of. Well now that we got that cleared up, I'm still waiting on my answer Gamble, as I said before I got paperwork and I'm too tired for this dance. There's that wit we all know and love. Alright Keys, to answer your question, yes I have the results that was requested by detective Stevens. Question before I tell you the results? It doesn't matter Gamble. What? I said it doesn't matter. Whatever question you are about to ask is just save it. All I want to hear is those results. As a matter of fact, I'll spare you the oxygen Gamble and just tell what I know the results are. Let me guess, you're going to tell me that the results came back with my prints or you found my blood on the murder weapon or something. Then after telling me this I'm supposed to ask surprise like I never saw that coming. We go back and forth for a while arguing and yelling, you know the usual. Then after a while you try to get me to calm down and wait for here it is you ready for it…tell me it's ok you can trust me I'll help you get through this. Stop me if I'm wrong Gamble. Oh no please continue. Thank you, now after supposing helping me, you're going to ask I need to know how you did it so I can help or something like that. You probably telling yourself he doesn't have any other play, we got his print and his blood on the murder weapon, well damn that should be case close right? Wrong, not with your ego Gamble, you need one more thing to boost your pride. Since you got it all figure out Keys, what may I ask is that one thing? This. (Gamble looks confuse) What? My tie? What the hell is my tie have to do with anything? Not your tie, it's what's behind your tie. You think I didn't notice you were wearing a bug. How the hell did you come to that conclusion? If there is one thing I know about you Gamble, if not the only thing, is that you're intensely superstitious. Everyone here knows that Keys It's not like I was hiding it. And everyone also knows that detective Gamble never wear anything black. It's not a racist thing it's just bad luck right Gamble? It's extremely bad luck, so let's hear it Keys, what was that one thing? A confession Gamble. You could of went to LT and Internal affairs with your little false positive files on me. As I said earlier, you got my suppose prints and blood on the murder weapon and add that with my history. C'mon Gamble that's slam dunk.

(Keys smile) But then that pride and envy in you is just boiling isn't it, you need more. I could go on, but this is just me thinking out loud, I'm told it's an annoying habit. Sorry to cut you off Gamble, what were you saying, something about the results?

(Gamble small giggles) Damn you again Keys. You should really get that paperwork done it's getting late. I'll see you in the mourning Keys, gets some rest. Yea you too, oh and Gamble! Yea? I liked that blue tie you wore last week, it looked good on you. (Gamble smiles) There it is again…fucking art. You have no idea how hard it was for me to put this thing on Keys, now I need a cleanse. (Gamble steps on tie) See you in the morning. (Next morning) Hey sorry I'm late. Long night Keys? Yea you can say that Monroe. Here's those report LT. Alight set them down over there. Don't get comfortable you two, go meet up with Rakes and Gamble. There with Doctor Lander in here atopy room. (groups gathers in room) So are we all here? How you doing Doctor? Mourning detectives, hope you had your coffee this morning because you're going to need your energy for what I have to show you. Hey where the hell is Gamble? Rakes he's your partner have you heard from him? No last time I heard from him was yesterday. His phone probably died or he overslept or something I'm sure he'll be here in a few minutes. That's a first, usually he's the first one at the district. Well he was with me last night, I gave him my conclusion on the wife's murder. He didn't tell any of us, typical, what was your findings doctor? He did tell me last night when I was filling out these reports. Basically the wife was killed the same way as Frank. Blow to the back of the head with the bolt gun, then drilled, then shot. Exactly right detective Keys. My findings indicated that the bolt gun was the initial kill shot, then the killer drilled the holes in the head and lastly shot her in the back of the head. (Monroe sighs) Exactly like

Frank was killed. Horribly, and gruesome, and to add injury to insults we still don't have a single suspect or motive. I'm still torn as to if this was a hit on the Steffens or maybe someone is trying to make a statement. After all Frank was a pretty wealthy man and has a lot of connections. You still thinking it about the money Monroe? What else is there Keys? You said it yourself money is still the number one motive for murder. Yea it is true. (doctor walks around) If I can interject, I may can help answer some of those questions. I ask you all here because I wanted to share what I found while doing the atopies on detective Stevens. That was fast, you did the atopy already. Yea detective Rakes, your lieutenant and I.A wanted this to be top priority. Can't disagree with that, after all he was a cop, so you were saying doctor? I discovered cause of death for detective Stevens. We were thinking some kind of poison. Not quite detective Monroe, the medical term would be called Hemolytic transfusions. It's very rare but to clarify, detective Stevens died from a wrong mixture of blood. I don't understand doctor, are you saying he died from tainted blood or something? (doctor stares around) I'm saying someone injected detective Stevens with type A blood and that was what killed him. To sum it up, Hemolytic transfusions is when your red blood cells attack the transfused blood when that blood doesn't match. Your immune systems attack's the blood cell ripping them apart triggering blood clots. Blood clots form in your vein and you died quit gruesomely. You said injected right doctor? I did, here look. I would have missed the injected site if I had not removed his tattoo. (Keys sighs with confusion) So the tattoo covered the injected site and we thinking the killer knew that. It's actually quite clever, it's a good thing you're the best at doing your job doctor Lander. Thank you detective Keys, I always take pride in my work. So you said he was killed by a mixture of blood. Do we know whose blood? Yes, and this is where it's going to blow your mind. Detective Stevens blood type is O+ and when I did the blood work on him I discovered he had O+ and AB-. I'm not seeing the mind blow part. Well detective Rakes, both Frank and Karen blood type is AB-. What? You're saying Stevens was killed by Franks and Karen blood? (doctor looks with focus) That's' exactly what I'm saying detective. Like I said it's rare but not plausible and that is what I'm putting in my report. All I can say is that whoever did this is smart and scary and also it takes some skill to pull something like this off. Yea I was just thinking about that doctor. You want to share with the group Keys? To get close to someone and injected them without them knowing, takes serious skill. Maybe someone clipped him from behind and then used the needle on him. Someone clipped a 190lbs cop from behind, yea. maybe but Stevens usually careful about his surroundings Rakes. I guess it's possible, but a little too easy I'm just saying. Which brings this down to two possibilities. Either he was clipped from behind like Rakes suggested or a more likely occurrence. (Monroe sighs) You're saying he knew the killer. To be comfortable with a person long enough to let your guard down. It would only make sense that you know them Monroe. Yea that makes more sense and it's more of a possibility. Hey doctor was the injecting site the only physical marking on Stevens's body? Actually it was the first thing I noticed when I was cleaning him. After I notice it I order a rush toxics screen and just got the results. I haven't done the full atopy yet, I thought you all might want to know about the blood as soon as possible. Yea, I have to say that defiantly woke me up this morning. Let me ask you something doctor, was there anything else in Stevens toxic screen? You mean any drugs or alcohol? No sir besides the transfused blood, detective Stevens blood was clean. You thinking he was dosed then injected Keys? I was, but then Lander just disprove that theory. Well if he wasn't dosed, could he have taken something or was slipped something then passed out? That would give the killer time to inject the blood. True, excuse me doctor Lander how long in your opinion will it take for the affects to take hold when someone injected the blood? (doctor shows confusion) It varies in everyone, but I would say a few minutes to half an hour maybe. Some transfusing are accidental, but in this case it was intended. So to better answer your question detective Monroe, I would say 5, 10minutes max. (Monroe cracks a smile) I see, so let's run the scene, what are we thinking guys? According to doctor Lander, Stevens was injected before I showed up at the Steffens house. Well how was he? Was he acting funny or adjective or anything? Easy Rakes and he was fine, we barely talked. The only thing he said he had something and wanted to show me and Keys at the same time. He didn't know Keys and I went to different locations and so we just stood there waiting on Keys. So the killer somehow subdued Stevens and injected him with the blood, but he wasn't dosed with anything. You got something Keys? (Keys stares down) Hey Rakes, Monroe how would you take me down without me knowing or feeling it for a few minutes? What? You heard me. You too doctor, how would you do it? I don't know. Me either. (Keys walks around) Well think about it, me and Stevens are roughly the same height and size and were both well train officers. It's not that easy to subdue someone like that. Ok, well for me if I couldn't dose you in time I'll find a way to knock you out. Exactly, there you go doctor, so how would you do it? If you were to clipped me over the head I would feel that, of course right? But there are no indications that Stevens was hit over the head. (Monroe smiles) Ok Hank, how would you do it? There are a few ways as to knock a person out for a while without there knowing. If he wasn't dose, then maybe he inhaled something. Chloroformed? Yea, but then I'm sure if Stevens was chloroformed he would have told us about it Rakes. So what are you saying Keys just get to it. I'm getting their ladies, just breaking it down for you is all. Monroe you said when you got to the Steffens house and meet up with Stevens he was fine right, nothing out the usual? Again with this Keys? Nobody saying anything just bear with me. Doctor Lander just said that it would have taken at least ten minutes after being injected for Stevens to sub come to the affects. Correct doctor? Ten minutes give or take that is what I said. All this tells us is that Stevens was knocked out and injected either before he himself showed up at the Steffens house. (Rakes side smiles) Or he never left the Steffens house and was knocked out and injected while he was their processing the as a supposed robbery. You're thinking inside man? I am Rakes. Well you and Monroe was here when we got the call about Karen's murder. Was Stevens that only one here processing the house when you two showed up? Well I wasn't really looking at everyone else's faces, I was focus on Karen's body. What about you partner can you remember who all was there? Not really just Stevens and the crime scene team. You see where I'm going with this Monroe? (Monroe nods and half smiles) You're thinking the killer impersonated a crime scene guy. I mean if you think about it, you're in a room processing it with crime scene, you're not going to have your guard up or anything. You're there just doing your job, just another day. You're right Keys it would be easy for someone to knock him out and inject the blood, he wouldn't have seen it coming. That still doesn't answer the question of how he did it. The Steffens had a pretty big house Monroe. It would be easy for the killer to catch Stevens in a particular room while the others were still processing somewhere else. The killer could have knocked him out somehow injected the blood and then slipped right back into processing the house. After all a crime scene guy would have some medical expertise on where to inject into a vein. I agree Rakes but were still missing the why and how? What do you mean? If that scenario you said was true, then why didn't Stevens say anything about being knocked out to us? Did he just forget to tell us, but then that doesn't make sense right? Oh I see, who wouldn't tell someone he was knocked out?

Exactly Monroe. I know I'm not a detective like you guys, but I have to admit the suspense and intensity is getting to me. Don't get ahead of me yet doctor, if my hunch is right then you're going to give us our how. Ok I'm listening detective. You already confirmed that Stevens wasn't dosed and other then the foreign blood his toxic screen was clean. That is true detective. I know you're still working on him doctor, but can you do me a favor? Can you check Stevens left wrist for me? More specifically below his palm. Below the palm? Yes, ma'am, just humor me. Ok detective? (doctor eyes widen) Mmmm what's this? Looks like a concentrated sunburn spot or something? Or something indeed doctor, you just told me my how. Well how about telling us Keys, cause Rakes and I are in the dark? (Keys smiles) How about I show you instead.

Rakes come over here for a minute. Oh great. Don't worry doctor Lander right here nothing bad going to happen to you. Well now after you said that now I am worried. Just stand right here for me and I'll get to my point. Monroe take out your phone and time this. Time what? Just when I say start hit start. Alright whatever you say to see where this is going. Rakes if you will stand right here please. Fine. Good now hold out your hand like you are going to shake mines. Now watch close as I go in for the hand shake. (Rakes stumbles and fall) What the hell Keys!!? Rakes just fell to the ground!!? Start the time! (click) Keys what the hell did you just do? I'm going to explain just give me a minute Monroe. Is she breathing doctor. (doctor checks) She still breathing. (Monroe sighs with relieve) Well Keys!? Calm down calm down…wait for it

Monroe. Wait for what, wait till Rakes dead? (Rakes Gasp) Rakes are you ok!? Yea, why wouldn't I be, what the hell happen!? That's a good question? Keys you want to explain now? First hit the clock and tell me how long that was? Four minutes. Do you see it now Monroe? (Monroe sighs angrily) Yea I do, but you could have just said that. Was that demonstration really necessary Keys? Somebody want to fill me in? Rakes what's the last thing you remember? What kind of question Is that? Standing next to you, waiting for whatever you were going to do. Come to think of it why the hell was I on the floor!? Most likely the question Stevens asked himself, but didn't think nothing of it at the time. Now I see where you're going detective Keys. (Keys smiles) You want to explain it to doctor. Detective Rakes you know were knocked out for about four minutes right? You're kidding me when that happen? It's true myself and detective Monroe both witness it. So what does all this tell us? (Monroe stares) Four minutes..., plenty of time for the killer to inject Stevens with the blood and slip out the house undetected. That explains that part, but how did you knock her out Keys? Special technique I learned. It's accentually just applying pressure to the right pressure point on the body. Why did you want to learn something like that? I tell you about it later Monroe. (doctor scoffs) All and all I can see why you asked me to check detective Stevens wrist detective Keys. A concentrated circular point on his wrists is the same circular point I notice now on detective Rakes wrist. What, where in the hell did this come from? Sorry about that Rakes. (Rakes scoffs) Well this all explains about 75% of our case but there are still some holes that need to be fill. Yea you're right, like how did the killer get Frank's and Karen's blood to begin with? (Monroe sighs with grieve) Yes, and more importantly why was Stevens killed in the first place? Other than the bolt gun did he know something else that the killer didn't won't him to tell us. Or was he just collateral damage and the killer is just tying up loose ends. Both are compelling arguments so let's see if we can get some answers. Let's close out this case, for Stevens. Wait ladies, before we head back, let's try and keep some of this information to ourselves. I'm sorry detective Keys, but your Lieutenant and I.A are expecting my report as soon as possible, I can't as a doctor withhold information. No I wouldn't dare ask you to do something like that doctor Lander, but you did say you weren't finish with your atopy, just work slow, I mean you are under staff right? Why Is keeping this to ourselves important Keys? Are you saying you don't trust our colleague? Not exactly Monroe, but you yourself said the killer could be working with us as a crime scene guy. We assume it was one person, but we don't know it could be more than one. (Monroe sighs) As hard as it would be to, believe that, something inside of me is agreeing with you. Rakes how about it can we count on your discretion for now? Well apparently I was just knocked so yea I'll keep this under wraps for now. (Rakes sighs) So what are going to tell Lieutenant and I.A? The truth, just keep the little detail under wraps for now. Something like that Rakes. More or less yea, detective Stevens was killed by the blood and that's all we know until doctor Lander finish her full atopy. Meanwhile we continue our investigation into the Steffens and now Stevens murder. Sound good to you all? It's good with me. Yea me too. Hope you know what you're doing Hank. (Keys half smiles) Yea me too…thanks again doctor Lander we owe you one. No problem be careful out their detectives. Thanks. (doctor sighs with anticipation) Detective Keys can you help me right quick? It's nothing hard just need help moving detective Stevens body to my table. Sure doctor, I'll catch up with you two later. Alright me and Rakes will head back and check in with LT. (Monroe and Rakes leave) Whenever you're ready to move him doctor just say the word. (doctor smiles) What I am ready for detective Keys, is the truth. Excuse me? You and I both know you missed that pressure point on detective Rakes wrists. (small laugh form Keys) I guess I shouldn't be surprise...so you notice that too? Well I have been a doctor for going on 20years, it's not a shock that I wouldn't know about pressure points on the human body. Fair enough doctor. So let's hear it detective, what was your real motive behind that little demonstrations? (Keys sighs) Two reasons doctor. As you know it's not unusual that this case was turning towards me. Throughout my entire life their always someone out there gunning for me. So to counterattack moment like that I took it upon myself to always have a contingency plan to every case I had. Weather I needed one or not, it was always there. Sounds like a lot of extra and sometimes unnecessary work detective. Call it my defense mechanism and when you have a generation like mines, it's best to have one. But tell me detective, how do you know when you need one? (Keys smiles) I guess you can say in certain cases I get I get a feeling or you can call it part of my annoying thing I'm told I do. Be that as it may doctor...you were one of my reasons for that demonstration. And as I expected your performance was flawless. Excuse me detective!? C'mon doctor you said it yourself you knew I intently missed that pressure point. So why don't you tell me? Why didn't you say anything then? (doctor signs) Good questions detective, and honestly I don't really have a good answer to it. I guess you can call it respect towards you. Yea I know the story about your generation and yet here you are still fighting the good fight. For me I never was the one to judge someone just because of their family history. So in that notion when you did your demonstration wrong I was curious. Then I noticed you glance at me.

Within that five second glance...I don't know something inside told me to trust you. And that right there is why I chose you doctor Lander. So how did you know I wouldn't say anything then? Did you gamble with whatever decision I would have made? Something of the sort, but all and all you can call it intuitions. I'll take that as a compliment detective Keys. It was intended doctor and after all I was right. What about the second reason? (Keys pauses) Detective Rakes. In the back of my mind I've always had a feeling about her from the beginning of this case. Just little things don't seem to add up with her. What are you saying detective, you surely not thinking she's the killer? That's impossible she's a cop after all. (Keys scoffs and smiles) Nothing impossible doctor. Doesn't matter who a person is or their profession. Everyone on this Earth is capable of being a killer. Certain people in certain professions are the hardest to prove to be a killer. No one ever notice or considers them until it's too late. Do you know why doctor…? Why? Because there are a cop. So what are you going to do next detective? (Keys sighs) I don't know yet, still working on it, but for now guess I'll get back to the case. Oh and doctor. I know detective this conversation never happened. Good to know I was right about you, looks like I owe you twice. I'll hold you to it, good luck detective Keys and again be careful. Always, and no need to worry doctor, after all… (Keys cracks a smile) I still have another contingency.

{**NARRITIVE**: In situations like this, do you know the one word that hardly ever gets a right answer to no matter how much you ask…? Why? That one word is hardly ever answer correctly to satisfy a person's need for redemptions. Think about it for a minute, you hear it probably everyday: Why today? Why now? Why this particular moment? Why I couldn't save this person? This one I'm sure everyone on Earth has said to themselves a few million times…why me? Now that can be a positive or negative but still why me? A person can drive themselves crazy asking why to everything. Trust me you're never be satisfied with the answer…just contented. The only thing you can do when you get the answer to one of your whys, is simple…you allow it to consume you or learn to live with it. Either or, will you be truly satisfy with the answer…? Exactly}. Hey you were in there for a little minute, is everything good? Yea doctor Lander is just under staff; just thought I'd give her little extra hand. What did you and Rakes found out with the LT. More or less the same thing. I gave him an update on what we found with Stevens and that we needed to head back to the Steffens to get some insights. I just gave him the important details. He and I.A are in his office talking now. (Gamble scoffs) Talking about what? Damn why you creeping around!? You're late, where you been? Not that I have to answer that Monroe, but I overslept and my alarm didn't go off. You overslept? Yea I overslept, I had a late night doing paperwork. I called you several times Gamble, I had to cover for you. Sorry about that Rakes won't happen again, but I appreciated it partner. Keys… Gamble. What's wrong with you two? Nothing Monroe, so what's are next play? I heard about Stevens, has anyone notify his wife and family yet?

No not yet Gamble, we figure we'll give them some closure by figuring out who did this to him. Yea that make sense, after all it's what everyone always ask for. So are we heading back to the Steffens house Monroe? Yea that's the plan, but I got a feeling where about to get an ear full from LT. Lieutenant. (LT walks up angrily) I'm not going to get into with you four today, I got more important things to worry about. Just tell me does anyone have something on this case? No, let me tell you what we have. We got three murders and no suspects. I got four of my top detectives standing right here in front of me with nothing, but their thumbs up their asses. Frank and Karen's murder is still front page and top story on channel four news. We got I.A poking around the district which is something we definitely don't need around here. (Gamble murmurs) wonder why? I'm sorry detective Gamble did you have something to say? No sir lieutenant. Good, cause like I said before I'm not in the mood. Now detective Monroe and doctor Lander filled me in on the cause of death for detective Stevens. What are you four thoughts? Monroe? I figure we go back to the Steffens house and try to retrace Stevens steps. Hopefully we find something crime scene missed. (LT nods and sighs) Keys? I agree with Monroe, but on the other side I think we need to figure out how the killer got a hold of Frank's and Karen blood in order to dose Stevens. (LT nods and sighs again) Hmmm Rakes? I want to be here with doctor Lander when she finishes her atopy. She's been under staff lately and I want to make sure that there are no other surprises with this case. I agree and what about you Gamble? I agree with

Monroe and Keys sir, and beside I've been cooped up at the district all throughout this case. I think it's best if I do a little leg work and help out Monroe and Keys. (LT scoffs) I see and you're right I think it's best if you get some air. So Monroe, you Keys and Gamble head back to the Steffens house and try to retrace Stevens step. We need to know where in the house he was injected. Yes, sir. Rakes you head back to doctor Lander and help her with the atopy. Hopefully she can tell us in better detail about the blood. Yes, sir. I said it before and I'll say it again, you four are my top detectives start acting like it. I won't this wrapped up before weeks out, now get to it. (LT walks away) You know that wasn't as bad as I thought. You expected more Monroe? Oh no I think I'll take that as a win. Keys you drive, I can use a power nap…you coming

Gamble? You're letting him drive, that's not like you Monroe. You never let anyone of us drive. Never thought of it like that, don't tell me you're jealous Gamble. It's just a short drive to the Steffens house, don't get so antsy. (Keys short snuffs) Something on your mind Keys? Nothing, still playing the envious card I see. Don't flatter yourself Keys and get off your high horse. Whatever you say...Oh and Gamble...nice tie, it looks good on you. (Gamble grunts and smile). Where are you going Keys, you missed the turn? Just roll with me for a second Monroe, in order to retrace Stevens steps, we need to head back to the beginning. The beginning of what? The first murder Monroe..., Frank Steffens. Why do we need to do that Keys? I don't think Stevens was injected at the Steffens house. Oh really and what's make you say that

Keys? Oh wait let me guess, intuition. Not exactly Gamble, we know Stevens was processing the Steffens house right? But I'm thinking Stevens would start from the outside in. I'm with Gamble Keys, what makes you say that? Frank was killed two block from his house in an ally and then place on 3rd and Maple. Stevens knew this from our report Monroe. So? So don't you think he would have started were Frank was killed and then worked his way to his house? Hmmm, I guess I can see where you're going with this. I guess we can start their too and hopefully we'll find something. Since you seem to know everything Keys, what exactly are we looking for again? We're looking for where Stevens was injected Gamble. So between Franks house and this ally, were supposed to figure out were Stevens was injected? Just a few blocks of trying to find something that we don't know what it is. Is that the gest of it Keys? No we'll be all day trying figure that out Gamble. I was thinking something you might enjoy. Let's recreated the scene, I think it will go faster that way. Recreating the scene sounds an all day job as well Keys. Yea but you're going to play the killer and I'll be Stevens. So you want me to kill you, I can do that. No just knock me out and inject me, either way you should still enjoy it Gamble. What about me, what am I supposed to do? I need your eyes Monroe. I need you to run the scene for up and tell us where between here and the Steffens house would be the best place to inject me. Ok I can do that. Alright let's get this started, Monroe call It out. Ok so our theory is that before detective Stevens came to the Steffens house he was here somewhere in this location. We assume he was here looking for some evidents or clues since this is where Frank Steffens was murdered. Frank was then moved to 3rd and Maple which is three block in the opposite direction of his house. So that tells us Stevens would go in the other way towards his house. Alright Keys start walking. Ok we are assuming at some point between here and Frank's house is where our killer enters the scene. We're also assuming that Stevens knew the killer. Why is that Monroe? Because according to doctor Lander, Stevens didn't have any marks on him indicating a struggle or being attacked. You would know this if you weren't late Gamble. Again with that Monroe? Anyways since we know Stevens wasn't attack, it's only common that he knew the killer. Or killers… we still don't know if these three murders were the doing one person or more than one. Yea that's true Keys, so let's just assume one killer for now then. Alright we made it to the Steffens house, now what Kelly. You tell me Gamble; you're playing the killer. Where would be a good place to knock Hank out and inject him without anyone noticing you. Well if it was me, somewhere secluded but not too out the obvious where it would get attention. Good to know Gamble. Just playing a role Keys. So now we assuming Stevens and the killer are talking around Frank's house about whatever. So boys, where around here is a good and secluded place. Somewhere I could get you alone Keys. You don't have to be so creepy with it Gamble. You asked me a question, I'm just giving you my opinion. How about in plain sight. You got something Keys? Yea look there. What is that, is that a door hitch? (Keys open the door? It's their cellar. Somewhere seclude, but not too obvious where it would get attention. Yea a cellar would fit that criteria. Yea good profiling Keys so why don't you two go and check it out, it's looks too cramp for all of us to go down there anyways. What's wrong with you Monroe, looks like you seen a ghost. Nothing Gamble, just not too good with close spaces that's all. (Keys smile) She scared of spiders. Oh thanks a lot Keys, remind me not to tell you anything else again. Look I have seniority so just go please and see if you get anything from that cellar. I'll check the perimeter out here, and see if I get anything. You got it boss lady. I can already hear that mocking in your tone Gamble. And by the way I'm not scared of spider, I hate spiders, so go down there and get bit in the ass please. (Keys smile) alright let's get this over with Gamble, let's go. Don't order me around remember I'm supposed to be the killer. Alright killer we got the location so let's test our theory. According to doctor Lander It would have taken at least ten minutes before Stevens sub come to the injection. Also he had to been knocked out for at least four minutes in order for the killer to inject him. How do you know that Keys? Oh right you weren't there. Me, Monroe, Rakes, and doctor Lander did a little experiment to get figure that out. Seems like I did miss a lot. No not really Gamble, but anyways we figured out Stevens was knock out for about four to five minutes. Ok I think I'm caught up now. So you want to see how long it takes for me to knock you out, inject you and then go back in the house to rejoin crime scene. Not completely Gamble, we assuming the killer was impersonating crime scene but he could have simply walked away after knocking Stevens out and injecting him. I'm not too sure about that Hank! Looks whose back, how's that suppose perimeter check Monroe? I was really hoping something bit you down their Gamble. You're saying you don't believe that the killer could have walked away, you must have found something. More or less Keys, look at that. What am I looking at? What the bird house? Yes, and no, it's what's in the bird house, look close. Well I'll be damn, it's a camera. Indeed, it is and I took it upon myself to hack in and check the footage. Well are you going to keep us in suspends Monroe, what you see? See for yourself. Well there Stevens as we expected, snooping around the Steffens backyard. And as we thought it would seem he has company. I can't make out the face. Of course you can't Gamble, did you really expected it to be that easy? The killer back is towards the camera but it just looks like there talking. Yea for now but look, it's about to get worse. Looks like Stevens heading back towards the house. Look there it is…the false handshake. And down goes Stevens, he didn't even see it coming. There he goes, killer injects Stevens with the blood. And now, there's your answer Keys, our killer doesn't walk away. Look at him, he's just standing over Stevens without a care in the world. This guy is cold. Which makes him even more dangerous to catch. How so Keys? A man with a cold heart is a man with nothing to lose. That's deep, almost poetic Keys. Do you ever take a day off from being an ass Gamble? What can I say Monroe, it's one of my traits. Look there, look like Stevens is waking up.

Completely unaware, looks like he our killer go back to talking. Look there, looks like Stevens heads back in the house and our killer simply walks away. It would appear not Keys. It would appear our guy is smarter than we thought, when he walks away he keeps his head down. Yea your right Monroe almost like he knows about the camera in the birdhouse. Something tells me he does. You thinking he put it there before all this Keys? I'm thinking a lot of things Monroe. (Gamble grunts) of course you are. Wait now he's heading back toward the door. Looks like he's leaning over, the hell is he doing? I do think you're right Keys. What's that supposed to mean? Seems like you know something we don't Monroe? Yea, what our guy was leaning over for. And you waited this long to tell us. Why didn't you just say that from the start Monroe?

Not now Gamble. This was under that pot by the back door, it's address to you Keys. (Keys stares intensity) (YOU'RE ALL THE SAME, EVENTUALLY THE OTHER FOOT WILL DROP, BUT BEFORE MY LAST BEATH... I'LL TAKE EVERYTHING FROM YOU...AS YOU ONCE DID). Well well, you want to tell us what that was about keys? I don't have time for your sarcasm Gamble. But to ease your mind, I haven't gotten the sightless clue believe it or not. One thing is true, our killer defiantly knew about that camera. (Gamble laughs) Are you fucking kidding me! What the hell is your problem Gamble? You steady amaze me Keys. You just got through reading, what is clearly a death letter toward you, and yet hear you are without a care in the world. I mean most people would have some kind of reaction but you...nothing.

Seems like you're the one with the problem Keys. Not a problem at all Gamble, what did you expect from me? He's got a point Gamble; I mean are you really surprised? Like Keys said what did you expect? Keys to freak out or something? I've been his partner for years, trust me it's just part of his thing. Oh I know all about it...believe you me Monroe. And it would also seem our guy just made solving this case a little easier. (Monroe smiles) Changing the subject, see what I mean Gamble? Why you say that Keys, you see something?

Maybe it's nothing, but look how our killer is walking away. I'm not seeing nothing. Look closer Gamble. Almost look like he has gimp in his walk. (Keys hesitates) Yea, almost like an injury. You're doing it again Keys, what's going on in that head of yours.

Nothing Monroe just thinking. About? About this letter. I've had my share of hate and dirty looks and people looking for a way to blame me for any and everything, you know the usual. But this letter is more than that, it sounds like pure hatred. That's something we can agree on Keys. When thinking back, have you ever taken something from anyone. I don't need this from you right now Monroe. I wasn't trying to insinuate anything Keys, just asking a question? Far as I know I haven't done nothing of the sort Monroe. You sure about that? Again with the sarcasm, I have to hear this from you too Gamble. Temper… careful Keys or you might have a heart attack. (Keys scoffs) so what's next? We take this tape back to the forensic lab and try and see if we can clean it up. We might be able to see our killer face. You might not care

Keys, but I really believe you need to look at that letter again. Maybe something will spark from the past. Yea that's what I'm worried about. Did you hear me Keys? Yea I heard you and I'll keep thinking on that Monroe. If you two are done, can we go, I don't need another ass chewing by the LT again. Yea good point, with what we've discovered it should keep him at bay for now. Key's you coming? Yea just had to check on something. Check on what? Can you get out of my business Gamble but, if you must know I was calling Rakes to see if she and the doctor came up with anything else with Stevens. Turns out there are still backed up, but should be through within the hour. Well before we head back let's run through the Steffens house. You two were already here before, didn't you already process the house. Technically yes and no Gamble.

The first time I was here it wasn't a crime scene, I was just questioning Mrs. Steffen and consoling her after her husband had been murdered. The second time was when I was told by the LT that Stevens wanted to speak to me. So you two never comb through the house? Like she said Gamble we never had a reason to. After Karen was murder Stevens was called in and had crime scene process the house. So on that note, why are we going through the house when crime scene already did? Why are you complaining so much Gamble, wasn't it you who said you wanted to do a little leg work? Well you got me there Monroe. Don't worry Gamble, since this is your first time here, about you be our fresh eyes? Whatever you say, you're the boss Monroe. We'll be in out, so let's start upstairs and work our way down. So what exactly are we looking for?

Anything unusual or out of place. How are we supposed to know what's unusual or out of place Monroe? This is the Steffens home, anything unusual or out of place might be normal to them. Hard for me to say Monroe, but I agree with Gamble. The only one who would know something like that would be there son and he's with CPS back with our protective custody. Aww that's cute, you two agree on something, then what do you suggest Keys? Before Karen's murder, she herself was a suspect in her husband murder correct? Yea, but we know she didn't do it because she regrettably was murder herself. I know, but hear me out Monroe. Stevens called you and me here because he found something here remember? You mean the bolt gun under the floor board? Exactly, but the question is, was it there before or after Karen's murder? Well we all saw the killer leave after dosing Stevens and Karen had already been murder. So if we are following your logic Keys, then the bolt gun was under the floor board before right? Not necessarily Monroe, remember what you said after you told Karen about Franks death. You said she took a walk towards Rosemary Park to clear her head. I remember, what are you getting at Keys? Always have to be drastic do we Keys? He saying after you two left the house our killer could have come back and put the bolt gun under the floor board. See how easy that was Keys, you could have just said that. He right Keys gosh. (Keys smile) well where's the fun in that Monroe? Idiot... let's head to the living room, that's where Stevens found the bolt gun. Is that the spot where Stevens found the weapon Monroe? Supposedly so Gamble. When I showed up here he was just standing there telling me to wait for Keys to get here. I didn't actually see where he found the gun, he just told us he found it under the floor board. Well that's not strange at all. Yea how did he know to look there in the first place? (floor creeks) Well there's your answer Gamble. That's convenience Monroe, but it still doesn't answer the question on when the gun was place there. That's true but I'm now thinking it was place there before Karen's murder. Oh really and how, pre-tell did you come to that conclusion Keys? Well because that camera that Monroe found in the backyard is fairly new, which means our killer must have put it there. Ok I'm not following Keys. Me either you lost me. Monroe how good is your memory? What!? Huh average? Look at that clock behind you. What about it Keys it's just a clock? Well for once it wasn't there when we all was here yesterday. Damn, now that you mention it your right Keys? And come to think, does that clock look out of place to you guys? I don't think it's weird, I mean people can put clocks wherever they want in their house Monroe. (Gamble chuckles) Hell I got one in my bathroom. That's stupid Gamble, but that's not what I'm talking about. Who the hell puts a clock in front of their TV instead of on top. I mean it's a complete eye-sore. That's because our killer put it there Monroe. We need to leave now! What's your deal Keys, what's wrong with you? I don't have time to explain Gamble, but for one thing that's not a clock…it's a camera. And for two look closer at the hands Monroe, see anything wrong? What the hell, the hands are ticking backwards. We need to leave now!!! (deep voice from the clock speaks) Leaving so soon detectives…but you didn't say goodbye. Please tell me I'm not the only one who heard that? No you're not the only one Gamble, seems like we fallen into a trap. (voice speaks again) Clever and sharp as always detective Monroe. But let me make something perfectly clear, as you three probably just notices, this clock you see here has a bomb place inside it. (Monroe scoffs) Damn it!! Well my friend it seems like you hold all the cards here? So let's hear it…what do you want? (voice speaks) Looks like you're in deep thought again… why don't you tell her what I want? (Keys silence chuckles) Of course…I'm flatter. It's ironic, seems like you plan this for, what I can image quite some time, and this is your ending just to blow us up? I mean apparently I took everything from you, and this is your ending for me? If this your revenge or whatever you want to call it, I have to say…

I'm disappointed. I would have more respect for you if you killed me face to face, cause at least then you'll have balls to look me in the eyes.

Keys what the hell, why don't you just tell him to blow us up now!?

Don't worry Gamble, if that was our friend intention, he would of blew us up the moment Monroe discovered those hands on the clock. (voice quietly laughs and speaks) Truly art detective. (clock starts ticking again)

Everyone out now!!! (5…4…3…2…1(loud explosion). (Few hours later) Can you hear me!? Sir? Detective can you hear me? Yea, not so loud, where am I? What happen? Calm down take it easy detective, you're at

St. Gabriel hospital, I'm doctor Rochelle. You were caught near an explosion, so you need to take it easy. Where are the others, are they ok? Yes, you all made it out safe, detective Keys and detective Gamble are in the next room being look over. You should count your blessing all three of you only sustain a few minor cuts. The last thing I remember was a loud explosion, I guess I must have blacked out. How did we all get here doctor? From what I was told it was your partner.

According to him before the explosions he manages to throw you and detective Gamble down a cellar that was nearby. (doctor chuckles) I'm glad you found almost being blown up funny doctor. Sorry detective Monroe it's not that, your partner just made me promise not to tell you.

Why the hell wouldn't I not want to know something like that, we were almost killed. No detective he told me not to tell you he threw you down a cellar...something about spiders. (Monroe smiles) That jackass.

Who a jackass, you talking about me again Monroe? Just can't get enough of me can you? See doctor I knew she always cared about me.

Not everything is about you Gamble. For a quick second I was almost worried about you, until now. (Gamble sighs) At least I got a second...I'll take that. Where is Keys, is he alright? Depends on your definition Monroe, look for yourself he's just standing there looking out the window. Go easy Gamble he going through a lot, I mean after all we were almost killed. And who fault is that Monroe, if Keys didn't taunt the guy we wouldn't be at this hospital in the first place. You don't know that Gamble, in my mind the killer was going to blow up the house regardless of Keys taunting. (Gamble grunts) I'm serious Gamble I mean if you stop and think about it, in blowing up the Steffens house the killer destroyed the cameras and any and all trace that was there.

She's right. Damn Keys you have to warn a person when you're going to sneak up on them. Wouldn't that defeat the purpose… (Keys cracks a smile) sorry about that Gamble. Hey partner how you feeling? Few cuts, but still here Keys. Good to hear, I'm glad you both are alright. Don't try and butter me up Keys, when this case is over with I'm slap you upside your head. So we just breaking promises now doctor

Rochelle? (doctor Rochelle smiles) sorry detective it just slipped out. What slipped out doctor? Nothing, she's busy Gamble. (doctor Rochelle chuckles again) Yea, I have to go and check on your results, I'll be back in a few minutes.

So where do we go from here guys? Not we Monroe…just me. How did I figure you would say something like that Keys? Sorry about that Monroe. Sorry… so what you think you're better than us. Oh course you do, Keys the lone wolf have to outdo everyone. Knock it off Gamble, in case you haven't realized it we were all almost killed, and I'm laying here with the world massive headache. So hearing you bitch for the ump ting time is the last thing I want to hear. No it's okay Monroe, I almost got you both killed so I deserve it. (Gamble grunts hard)

Listen, why don't you both just get some rest, Lieutenant and IA are most likely on their way here. What about you what are you going to do Key? I got a lot going on and I don't need to put anyone else in danger. Keys we been partners for a long time so I get the gest when you're lying. Don't worry partner I'm just going to get some air. Even I know that's lie, you're going after the killer aren't you Keys? I know me and you might not see eye to eye on things Gamble, but for once can we not argue. I just need you to trust me on this. You asking me to trust you Keys, give me a reason? Because…I know who the killer is. (Monroe and Gamble stare intensely) I know you both have a lot of questions, but I can't answer them right now. (long pause) Fine. That was a little unexpected Monroe. I agree with Gamble, that was usual for you. What can

I say Gamble, you might not trust him but I trust my partner. I appreciate that Monroe. So what are you going to do Keys, I take it when you were staring out that window a few moments ago, that brain of yours sparked something? Yes, and no Gamble, I guess I'll find out when I get there. And where is there Keys? I don't know yet, like I said before just need to get some air and think. I don't know, maybe I'll head to the park, I heard feeding the duck is relaxing. You two get better I'll see you around. You got a weird partner Monroe, and did he just say he was going to feed some ducks? What you call weird I call the usual Gamble, trust me it's just another day for Hank Keys. {**NARRATIVE**: Patients is truly a virtue. A lot of us have very short patients, while others patients is just their middle name. Everything in this universe has a twin so to speak; Light has it dark, happy has its sad, anger has its joy, and patients has its revenge. But patients has another side to it, and that would be choices. Good or bad the choices we all make are our own, it's the choices we make that define our past and present and form our future. It's all tied into a single repeated question in your head… what will you do? Fight or walk away, get revenge or let it go. You ask yourself will whatever we choose fix this pain or is it just a bandage…a temporary fix to the worlds bullshit. I guess that's irony to what we call life, everything we say and do all start with a question you ask yourself. So you tell me what will you do…choose?} Hey Keys I heard from LT that you, Monroe and Gamble were caught near an explosion at the Steffens? What the hell are you doing here? You should be still at the hospital?

I actually hate hospitals. Really Keys you almost got blown up and you can be bother to stay at the hospital until you get better? It's all good Rakes, just a few cuts the doctor already cleared me. What about Monroe and Gamble, how are they? There good, everyone is good, we were all lucky we got out with only a few cuts. That some luck Keys. Call it what you will Rakes, why are you still here this late? You still helping doctor Lander? Yea, everyone called it a day and went home and I.A, the doctor and LT all went to the hospital where Monroe, Gamble and you're supposed to be. I was going to head to the hospital myself but I figure I should show up with some good news. I'm just racking my head trying put this case together. Finishing up some paper work on Stevens, trying to catch up on things. Hmmm, so where are we with the case? Still can't get a beat on you Keys, you almost died and the only thing you're worry about is where are we with this case? It's this case that got me here in the first place Rakes. It's this case that put Gamble and Monroe in the hospital. It's this case that has gotten three people killed already. One of whom was detective Stevens, so please excuse my inpatients if wanting to end this. Alright easy Keys, the veins in your forehead is starting to pop, but I agree this case has taken its toll on everyone. But to answer your question, we really haven't made any luck. Other than what we all know with Stevens and the blood, we're at a standstill. What about the kid? He still with CPS and he has Hobbit with him for protection, so he's good. Hobbit huh? Yea, he said he could use the overtime so LT assigned him to watch over the kid. At least we have something good go our way. What about you Keys, other than the explosion did you guys found anything at the Steffens? As a matter of fact, we did Rakes. We found out where Stevens was attacked and injected. How you find that out? Turns out our killer put a camera in a birdhouse in the back-yard. Well that's new, putting a camera in a birdhouse have to say that's a first for me. I take it you were able to see everything on it? Not everything we were only able to see Stevens being attacked. That's good, well bad choice of words, but then you must have seen the killers face? Is it ever that easy Rakes, no we couldn't get a clean shot of his face. It doesn't matter now, everything we discovered got blown up in the explosions. Speaking of explosions Keys, how did that happened? I don't know Rakes you tell me? Excuse me…what the hell that's supposed to mean Keys? I mean ever since this case started it seems like you were always…in the back ground so to speak. Started at the park when everyone split up. You were right there being all friendly, trying make me believe I could count on you anytime. Isn't that right Rakes? Then fast forward after I question Frank Steffens partner, I'm thinking LT didn't have you tail me, but that was your plan all alone wasn't it? And now here we are again. (Rakes cracks a smile) I think that explosion is taken its toll on you Keys, what exactly are you trying to say? Like I said before why don't you tell me Rakes? Well if I didn't know any better it almost sounds like you think I'm involve somehow? I'm thinking a lot of things Rakes I mean you know me? No, actually I don't know you Keys. No one here even actually know you if I'm being honest. Is that a problem Rakes? Not for me, but it makes those walls of your steel instead of brink. What's your point?

My point is having those kinds of walls up you're going to have eyes on you. That's not new to me Rakes. I've had eyes on me since I was fifteen, moving around from foster home to foster home because nobody wanted anything to do with me. So don't stand there and lecture me on walls being put up. (Rakes sighs) You know you're right I guess I'm the last person here to judge someone, when I myself grow up quite well, so I apologize Keys. Changing the subject are we Rakes…

(Keys scoffs) it doesn't matter. Hey where are you going? You said it yourself Rakes, maybe that explosion has taken a toll on me, think I might get some air. Mind if I join you? You don't need my permission, after all aren't you suppose to keep an eye on me? Are you still on that Keys, I was just doing my job. So am I Rakes. Why are we here of all places? What? What's wrong with the park? Seriously, oh nothing it's just the park where Karen Steffens was murdered and you don't see nothing wrong with that Keys? Well now that you mention it, I guess it is a little disturbing. So why are we here then Keys? (Keys smiles grizzly)

Just trying to set-up the right time and moment for you to come out?

(Rakes looks confuse) It was sort of funny the first few times but now, keys you need help. I told you I was just doing my job if you're still thinking I have anything to do with this you're insane? Sorry Rakes I guess I should have been more clear, but I wasn't exactly talking to you.

Now I know that explosions is affecting your brain. In case you haven't notice we're the only two out here. (Keys side smiles) Is that right…so are you just going to stand there or are you waiting for a better moment!? Who are you talking to Keys!? Don't think you'll get a better moment then this… doctor. (doctor smiles and laugh lightly) My my…truly art indeed…hello detectives. (Rakes gasps in shock) Doctor Lander!? Is that you? Yes, it seems I forgot to thank you detective Rakes.

Your help was much appreciated. What are you talking about? What are you doing here? It's quite embarrassing, as your partner stated I really was waiting for the right moment. Right moment for what? (Doctor walks towards Rake) Sorry detective I really did appreciate your help, but it's not needed anymore. What!? What are you talking about? What are you doing? Shhhh (Rakes falls down) How's that detective, was that the right pressure point or do you think she's faking again? So you knew? As I told you before I know a thing or two about pressure points. It seems you do doctor, so where do we go from here? Is the part where you go in a speech and tell me about how I did something to ruin your life? Afterwards killing me to fulfill your revenge gluttony. (Doctor laughs) Revenge!? (Doctor shoots Keys in shoulder) No this has nothing to do with revenge detective. Is more of a death bed promise. (Keys starts heavy breathing) There's that 22 we were looking for. So I killed someone close to you is that it…I see. (doctor glares) No you don't, not even close, this has nothing to do with you per say. This has to do with your generation of murderers. And here I thought you said you didn't judge me for my past doctor. I stand by what I said detective, all these years I've been watching you and you never harmed or killed anyone. But we all know that other foot will drop eventually. (Keys grunts) Years huh? So you're going to kill me before that inevitably happens? So that what you meant Stevens…have to say I didn't see it coming either. I don't know what you're mumbling about, but you're actually telling me you surprise detective… you? First time for everything doctor. At least we can agree on that detective. You have no idea what the word patients means. Every time, every moment I saw you I had to literally hold my breath. (Keys scoffs) So there is a speech, so why don't you tell me what exactly did I do to you? I'm not being an asshole, but all this seems to be a little extreme to be just simple revenge doctor? Actually it was something you had no control of…you were born. So everything you've done was because I was born. More or less yes detective, and even more of a reason, you weren't supposed to be born. You talk as if you know me doctor? (doctor smiles) In a way I guess you can say that... after all…I was there. You were where? I was right there detective…right there in that delivery room. (Keys stares with shock) I waited twenty-eight years to see that look on your face detective. It's the same look I had the first time I looked into your eyes in that delivery room. If that how you felt than why didn't you just kill me then!? Why wait all these years? Well I'm sort of offended detective, for one I'm not a savage, after all you were just a baby. But I do have to admit, it took every fiber not to just kill you right there. Then you should have. Well to ease the urge, I did kill someone else that was there. (Keys grunts with pain) My mother…? Yes, detective I took her from you, but trust me it was for the better. Oh don't give me that look, after all you saw the video right, she turned her head and told us to get you away from her. So you had to kill her? Just gave her a little injection and then my work would be done. But then as you know there is always something right? And that something just happened to be you. (Keys still grunt with pain) You're still not making sense doctor, what the hell did my mother do to you? And on that note, I didn't ask to be here, but you somehow you have this intents hatred towards me? (Doctor angrily stares) You're not listening detective, I don't have hatred towards you per say... just your generation. Well I don't have anything to do with my generation. You have everything to do with your generation!!!! Every male in your line from your great grandfather down to your worthless father are all mass murders. You only know the gest detective but me, I have the pleasure and pain to know it all. Know what? Your great grandfather and grandfather both killed over twenty-five people in their life-time. No one knows why they went on their murder spree, but after that they spawn son's. Those sons of theirs also became mass murders. I know this because of those sons was your father. (doctors stares with intents anger) ... Your father slaughter my entire family. My mother, my father, my little brother and both my grandparents. I would have been killed as well, but that night I happen to be at night school getting my degree. That day I looked into all my family's eyes and made a promise that I would get revenge, no matter how long it took. A few months later after becoming a doctor, I got a call to work. A woman was in labor and I guess the rest is history. After learning who that woman was everything in me snapped…and It was in that moment after seeing your eyes, I broke my promise. Guess I wouldn't say I broke it more or less added to it. I promised myself that I would take everything I could from you. Your smile, your peace of mind, your freedom, your job, and after there was nothing left to take…your life. Never the less you were just a baby, so I started with your mother. After that I track down your worthless father, you should have seen the look on his face when I told him who I was…the joy on my face. That's quite a story doctor, I take it I'm supposed to be angry. Killing my parents for revenge, I'd have to say I would have probably done the same thing. (doctor laughs) There it is again that unfeeling thing of yours. I have to say now I didn't see that coming. Seems like we're all caught off guard these days. (Keys stands in pain) You still haven't answer my question doctor, why wait all this years? I guess you can say I wanted to give you a chance, but really it was the challenge. What challenge? The challenge of a perfect kill. Even you have to admit detective, a worthy opponent is one hell of a high. And it's that high that's intoxicated, it makes you crave it more and more. Now I see, you're right doctor it wasn't revenge so to speak that lead you to kill my parents. It was the kill itself. (doctor cracks a smile) That right their detective is why you are a worthy opponent. Yes, you're right I don't know what it was, but when I first saw your beautiful, baby brown eyes, that high rush through my body. (doctor laughs) I can say with great pride that I became obsessed with the kill detective. I could go on and on about this, but I do have somewhere to be. Your partner here should be waking up soon, so before I kill you I have to know, its' been eating at me for a while. (Keys sighs) How did I know you were the killer? Yes, I was sure I was careful and I know I didn't make any mistake, but it would seem I have. Excuse the slow start, I mean I was just shot. Its' just a flesh wound detective you'll live, trust me I'm a doctor after all. First mistake; that little demonstration of mines, was planned from the start.

So detective Rakes really did fake? Yea, but it wasn't for me, it was for you. I wanted to see if you would catch my so call mistake... and I was right you did. Second mistake was what I discovered on what I assume your birdhouse camera at the Steffens house? (doctor nods her head slightly) I remember a conversation we had a few days ago, you were explaining what a bolt gun was remember? I do recall that conversation detective. Then you should also recall that injury to your leg you told me about. (doctor scoffs) The camera caught me walking away and you notice the gimp in my steps. Guess I should have figure that out. Was that all my mistakes? No, there were two more that convince me you were my killer. The first one was that bug you planted on Gamble's tie. How'd you figure that out detective? Well it wasn't the bug itself, it was what Gamble said that I knew it was you. After arguing with him back and forth for some time, before he left Gamble called the thing I do truly art. Now fast forward to when me, Monroe and Gamble was back at the Steffens house combing through it again. That clock with the voice camera in it, I'm assuming that was you as well. You said to me, before you tried to blow us up, truly art detective. Now call me crazy, how could you have known to say that unless you heard it before? (doctor laughs) Damn you detective Keys and I mean that, you are truly something else. Well I enjoyed our little conversation, but as I stated before I got somewhere I have to be. (Keys smiles with pain) Sorry you're going to cancel that little get together with Mr. Styles. (doctor scoffs with anger) What's the matter doctor? You're telling me you surprise…you? It looks like she's a little confuse…why don't you explain to her partner!? I guess that wound is taken its' toll on your brain detective…detective Rakes is still unconscienced. He was talking about me bitch!! (doctor sighs with fear) Detective Monroe…what are you doing here? What does it look like, I'm helping my partner and by the way thanks Keys. I take it you got my message at the hospital? Yea, it took a minute, but I figure it out and also took care of that little erring for you. Look at that you were right Keys; she does seem shocked. Let me clarify it for you doctor, my wounded partner here had a concerning feeling about Jacob Styles, so I did a little digging. Turns out Mr. Styles had a few hard marriages in his days and it also turns out that you doctor Lander was his first wife. And not to go into detail, but after putting the pieces together we needed to drive you out...so here we are. And by the way to better clarify my partners earlier statement. The reason you need to cancel that get together with Mr. Styles is because he's dead. (doctor gasps with shock and anger) You bitch, you killed him? No, after the evidence mounted up on him and his role in the murders of Mr. and Mrs. Steffens, he took his own life. You did this didn't you, this has you all over Keys! Actually doctor believe it or not he confessed everything on a tape that was sent to me. He tells us everything in detail, after confessing everything he put a bullet under his chin. (Keys sighs with grief) Damn you Styles, I didn't think you would go that far. I know, but he said something about a right he had to wrong with you Keys. There is something I still don't get doctor, why kill the Steffens? I don't think I have to answer anything you ask detective Monroe you're not a part of this. It was for me Monroe. It was her sick little challenge for me to solve. She killed two innocent people and detective Stevens all for what, some damn game for you to solve? She just doesn't get it does she detective? Get what, that you're a psychopath? That me and your partner are connected. Me, I got the bug, the absolute high for killing, and you partner has that something inside him that makes him my opponent. What can I say it's almost like we're twins of Fate. (sirens approaching) Looks like you're out of time doctor. (doctor starts to giggle) I disagree detective Monroe. (doctor holds a trigger) Put your gun down detective Monroe or I'll blow us all up, don't think I won't hesitate. Well isn't this familiar, this is the second time you put me in this situation Keys. (Keys smiles with pain) Sorry about that Monroe, guess this is my atonement to wash some of the blood from my generation. How noble, It would appear you didn't see this coming detective. It would seem that thing of yours isn't as sharp as I would have hope. I Guess it's sort of poetic, this all started with a tragedy bring you to me, and now it ends in a blast of glory…to bad I'm sort of disappointed detective. (Keys cracks a smile) Well lets' not disappoint her…Benson!! (loud gunshot) What the hell Keys, you were cutting it a little close wasn't it? Sorry about that Benson, but she was right, she did catch us off guard. Hey how you doing, you want to fill me in on what the hell just happened? Oh sorry Monroe, I had Benson here tail me just in case something like this happened. Why? Because other than being

Franks business partner, Mr. Benson here serve in the army with me. What!? Yea, I had the same responds when I first meet him too detective Monroe, I didn't recognize him. But when he showed up the second time I realize who he was. I knew who he was when he introduced himself to me the first time I questioned him, he said his last name first. What does this have to do with you being here now Benson. When we were in the Army we gave our unit a safe word, and this word meant one or two things. Either; you're being followed or tail me. Well…what was the word? (Benson smiles)…Shadow. Don't read too much into it Monroe, it's just an Army thing. Believe it or not Rodgers was the first one to use it. Are you kidding me Keys…Rodgers too? Yea, I know, but it's true. The second you know was Benson here when I came to him the second time. The last one was from detective Stevens before he died. Stevens too…? So when he whispered in your ear, he gave you the word? Yes, ma'am. And I'm assuming that call you made wasn't really you calling Rakes? No I was calling Benson, to give him the word. (doctor coughs up blood) Seems like you were always two steps ahead detective? Damn she took a bullet mid-center to the chest, and she's still alive. I have to say Keys she's a tough one. Sorry doctor if it wasn't for my family's generation you would have never gone down this path of murder. Save you sympathy, my path was my own choice, your family just happen to give me a reason. Geese even after being shot and now dying she still a bitch. It's not her fault Monroe, even though she doesn't accept it I still take some responsibility for her doing. Speaking of detective

Keys, you never told me the second part that convinced you? (Keys sighs) It goes back to a conversation I had with Rakes and the last thing I told you after our little conversation. I told her in everything I do with a case I always have a contingency. Mr. Benson here was that contingency doctor. (doctor quietly laughs) There it is, that perfect high...truly art...detective. So she's finally dead, serves her right, all this killing over revenge. Talk about obsession. No Monroe she wasn't obsess with revenge for me, while not for most, she was obsess with killing. That doesn't make any sense Keys, it's just creepy. It's true ma'am, me and Keys seen it ourselves while serving. Some people just get hooked on the kill, once they taken a life they want to do it again. (Rakes catches her breath) Why does my head hurt so much. What the hell happen? Keys, where's doctor Lander and what happen to you, are you shot? (Keys crack a smile) Rakes take a breath, calm down. Long story short, doctor Lander is our killer, she knocked you out and shot me and was about to blow us all up again. Benson here killed her before she could kill us, case close. (Rakes sighs heavily and stares blankly) Can we go to the hospital now… I got a headache. [FOUR MONTHS PASSES]

Knock, knock, surprise you still here? I thought you hated hospitals Keys? Still do Monroe, but I figure I can use the down time. What are you doing here? Just checking in on you making sure you're good. Preciate that partner. You know it's kind of weird, I asked the front desk clerk what room you were in and I went there and it was empty. So I have to ask, what are you doing here and who is that? You mean you don't recognize him Monroe…look closer. (Monroe eyes widen) Is that who I think it is Keys? It is…detective Monroe allowed me to introduce you to one detective John Hobbs. Oh trust and believe I know who he is Keys and you shouldn't be in here. (Keys smiles) detective Hobbs was found in the wood near an old cabin were it seems he was dead. Luckily a lumber jack man discovered him and got him to this hospital just in time. The doctors here were able to counteract the poison in his system, but the doctors had to induce a coma to keep his brain from suffering any more damage. I know the story Hank, but do you also know what they say he did? I would think after our previous indications you wouldn't be the one to judge someone so quickly Monroe? (Monroe sighs) Well I guess you got me their

Keys? So you never answered my question, why are you here? It's not nothing to concern yourself with, but I'm here to read him a book. Read him a book...you're kidding me!? I can see how that might throw you Monroe, but not only can I relate to Hobbs in a way, he's my mentor. What!? Yea, it was Hobbs who got me into a good foster home after bouncing around from one to another. And after I graduated the academy, he was the one who taught me everything there is to be a detective. You know what Keys, now that doesn't surprise me, now I see where you get it from. I just come here once in a blue moon and tell him what's been going on. No your good Keys, don't have to explain anything to me that's your thing. What you got there Monroe? This, just another case, but don't worry I told LT that you still had some le-way.

Besides I got Rakes and Gamble with me today. That's good, just another day at the office Monroe. The cycle never stops Keys, anyways I'll let you get back to, you can join us when you feel up to it. Thanks Monroe, and hey I really do appreciate you…I mean that. (Monroe smiles) Anytime, you'll warm up to me eventually partner and maybe learn you can trust me. (door closes) Hey how you doing Hobbs, it's me again, it's Hank. It's been a crazy few months and I'm sorry I haven't been here as much as I should. It's one of my regrets, but how are you, only God knows what's going on in that head of yours. I don't think I ever told you this before, but if it wasn't for you I most likely would have been dead a long time ago. So appreciate that and with that being said I'm going to do everything in my power to clear your name. So when you wake up you'll be a free man, I'll take on your burden. I got plenty of it, so one more won't kill me it's the least I can do for you. Now with that out the way I won't be reading you a book, but how about a story. (keys pulls up a chair) I got a good one that I know you will like and can relate to. I'm not going to tell you about the time I almost died, but rather (Keys smiles with pride) …I want to tell you about the time I should of die.

{**NARRATIVE**: Time waits for no man… in case you don't know that's a quote from Lincoln. Time, Patients, judgement, revenge, choices, regret and dedication. These are all what makes a person who they are and dictates their life. There the twins of the Sins so to speak, at least that's what I believe anyways. After all these years as my partner I can say with a great pride that I will never be able to do that something that Hank...Keys... does. Look at me, I'm starting to even talk like him...guess he's rubbing off on me. It's his gift I suppose, to be able to do what he does and do it with a smile. I've got to say it's one unique thing even you can't deny that. (Monroe smiles) But fucking annoying...Right?]

CPSIA information can be obtained
at www.ICGtesting.com
Printed in the USA
LVHW011202260122
709311LV00002B/77